TICKETS

The Kalamazoo City Dome. The city's brand-new family attraction was every bit as awesome and spectacular as Mayor Edward Saunders promised it would be: "A world-class entertainment center for a world-class city." Only thirteen months after it was announced, the KC Dome was complete. And with the doors about to open for the first time, all of Kalamazoo was bursting with pride.

It wasn't always that way. For months, everyone from editorial writers at the *Kalamazoo City Krier* to

street-corner cranks had been squawking about the extravagant building and its lousy location. Hardly anyone believed the mayor would pull it off. Who ever heard of an indoor-outdoor amusement park with a retractable roof? Why would anyone try to build one on top of the landfill in the southwest corner of the city? What parents would want to take their kids to the worst part of town? How would Kalamazoo City possibly afford such a boondoggle?

Of course, the project had its supporters. The mayor's inner circle was thrilled that the Dome would be even larger and more impressive than anyone had imagined. And throughout the brouhaha, Mayor Saunders never once wavered, even though his reputation and his legacy were on the line.

Now the KC Dome was finally opening, (almost) on time and (mostly) on budget. And Kalamazooians, young and old, rich and not-so-rich, had buried their differences and come out en masse for the big celebration. Even the project's noisiest critics were on hand. All of them had been waiting in line for hours, know- ing this day would go down in history.

The city officials were arrayed on a platform just outside the main entrance. The Kalamazoo City Coronet Club was there too, their horns announcing the big moment with a noisy fanfare as Mayor Saunders cut the ribbon and declared the Dome open for business. The wrought-iron gates whisked apart, and in a flash, the complex was crammed with eager fun-seekers and adrenaline junkies.

A huge crowd jostled to be among the first in line at the ScreamerCoaster, a roller coaster that swooped at such steep angles, you were almost guaranteed to lose your lunch. Kids of all ages swarmed for a chance to ride on Booooiiiiing!, a bungee jump that sent them flipping through the air. The crowd was buzzing with anticipation for the first of the nightly fireworks displays.

But everyone agreed that the finest attraction of all—the one that would be best remembered by everyone who saw it—was the Kalamazoo City River of Dreams, a ride through Kalamazoo City's fabulous history, featuring some of the most fantastic animatronics ever seen, and created by a top-notch team of artists and engineers direct from Hollywood. The line for that ride snaked throughout the floor of the Dome.

Within the sea of thrill rides, food stands, and ticket booths, a young couple held hands and marveled at the thrilling scene.

"Want another bite of cotton candy?" offered the boy, a good-looking, fresh-faced teen. He didn't need the red fur and bushy tail to be considered a fox; he was just that good-looking.

"No, thank you, Blake." The girl, a striking young platypus, pulled her boyfriend's varsity jacket closer around her chest as she rested her head on his shoulder. Tonight their hearts beat in rhythm as they celebrated the six-month anniversary of their first date.

"Hey, Vanessa, let's go check out the sKCy Scraper!" Blake motioned toward the Ferris wheel, its lights dancing in the reflection of his eyes.

"Honey, you know how I feel about heights."

"Oh, come on. Wouldn't it be romantic?" Blake smiled sweetly.

Vanessa looked from her boyfriend to the gigantic revolving wheel. "Okay. But seriously—if I say we're getting off, we're getting off."

"You got it, sweetie," said Blake. "This is going to be great. If there's any night to see the city from up high, tonight's it. Besides, I have a special surprise for you."

Vanessa followed him toward the towering machine, growing more nervous by the minute. By the time the safety bar was locked down, her heart was beating at a frantic pace. She smiled weakly as she leaned into Blake's shoulder and squeezed her eyes shut. The ride operator threw his wing in the air and gave a whistle, and the gondola holding the young couple lurched forward, rocking back and forth as it lifted off the ground. Vanessa's webbed fingers clutched Blake's shirt. He placed his paw around her shoulders and held her tight. Soon they were gliding up into the air, the wind gently tousling their fur. At that moment, the amusement park's massive dome began to retract, and they found themselves beneath a canopy of starlight. The city lights shimmered off the water, and the sound of the revelry below disappeared as they climbed higher into the sky. They rose quickly to the very top of the skcy scraper until there was nothing but air around them.

Everything was going just as Blake planned. With any luck, they would soon be basking in the glow of the fireworks display. "Vanessa, these past six months have been incredibly special. . . ." Blake shifted and reached into his back pocket. Vanessa's eyes widened.

"I made you this ring in shop class." Blake opened his paw. Inside was a shiny bronze hoop. It caught reflections of the neon lights below.

"Oh, honey," she said, looking up into his eyes. "It's beautiful!"

She leaned in to kiss Blake, but then, suddenly, the power in the Dome went out. The ride jolted to a stop, sending their gondola rocking back and forth like a frenzied pendulum.

Vanessa screamed.

Blake fumbled the ring, sending it plummeting down to what was then a pitch-black sea of chaos. Before he could offer a word of comfort, the shrieks of thousands of terrified revelers below drowned him out.

That's when the fireworks display began. But without power, the metal dome covering the park could not finish retracting. Fireworks exploded into its hard surface and burst into flames. The crowd's shouts of confusion turned into screams of terror as sparks and debris rained down on them.

Welcome to Kalamazoo City, home of the Disaster Dome.

KALAMAZOO CITY KRIER

Walden Pond Press is an imprint of HarperCollins Publishers.
Walden Pond Press and the skipping stone logo are trademarks and
registered trademarks of Walden Media, LLC.

Platypus Police Squad: The Ostrich Conspiracy
Copyright © 2014 by Jarrett J. Krosoczka

Library of Congress Cataloging-in-Publication Data
Krosoczka, Jarrett.
The ostrich conspiracy / Jarrett J. Krosoczka. — First edition.
pages cm. — (Platypus Police Squad ; [2])
Summary: "Detectives Rick Zengo and Corey O'Malley investigate
foul play at the opening of the Kalamazoo City Dome, the world's
largest indoor amusement complex" — Provided by publisher.
ISBN 978-0-06-207166-8 (hardback)
[1. Platypus—Fiction. 2. Amusement parks—Fiction. 3. Mystery and
detective stories.] I. Title.
PZ7.K935Ost 2014
[Fic]—dc23
2013047721
CIP
AC

Typography by Tom Forget
14 15 16 17 18 CG/RRDH 10 9 8 7 6 5 4 3 2 1
❖
First Edition

FAT CAT

ANIMAL CIRCLE

ALVIN AND STUFFY

NEAR SIDE

THE ZENGO HOUSE, 7:04 A.M.

"Firefighters were immediately on the scene and quickly doused the flames. Nobody was seriously injured, but the city has been shaken." Max Pearson, the on-the-scene reporter for Channel Five's *Action News*, stood in front of the smoldering Dome.

"More orange juice, sweetie?"

"Mom, c'mon, I'm watching!" Detective Rick Zengo gently pushed his mother aside so he could see the television screen, then caught himself. "I mean, no, thank you, Mom. It's just that this . . ." He motioned toward the television.

"I know. It's your job. I think it's so cute that you're a real member of the Platypus Police Squad!"

Zengo narrowed his eyes at her and turned the volume up. He had been a full-fledged detective for months now, and yet everyone still insisted on calling him "rookie," "tiger," "slugger." Even the guys at the station. It was fine at first, but these days it was really starting to break his bill.

"We reached out to the firm that built the Kalamazoo City Dome, but they refused to comment," continued Max Pearson.

"Probably because Maurice Robertson is a hack!" Zengo's dad barely looked up from the sports section.

"Dad, come on, just because he was hired by the city . . ."

"Ricky, I've known Maurice for years now. He didn't deserve the chance to draw up plans for the Dome, much less build it. *Anything to save a buck*—that's his motto. I could have told you the opening night would turn into a fiasco."

Zengo wondered what made his dad think *he* was such an expert on building amusement parks. His dad built kitchens for a living, not state-of-the-art roller coasters. As Zengo looked back at the TV, though, he

2

had to admit his dad had expertly mounted it beneath their cabinets.

"We're here now with someone who was stuck atop the so-called sKCy Scraper, one of many rides that was dangerously stopped midcycle when the park's systems went haywire," said Max Pearson. "Tell me, young lady, what was it like being trapped so high up and in complete darkness?"

"It was terrifying," she said.

Zengo nearly spit his orange juice all over the table. He recognized the girl before her name appeared on the screen. It was Vanessa O'Malley, his partner's daughter. Her boyfriend, Blake, the high-school football star, was by her side.

The image of two kids stuck atop the Ferris wheel had gone viral overnight. It had already become a symbol of the disastrous opening of the Kalamazoo City Dome. But Zengo hadn't realized it was O'Malley's little girl.

Vanessa continued, "We were stuck up there for *two hours* before these jokers got the power going again."

"It was pretty awful," Blake added. "My girlfriend

here is terrified of heights, but I thought it would be safe to take her up on a Ferris wheel."

"Clearly, you were wrong." Vanessa's arms were crossed.

Zengo recognized the fury in her eyes. It was the same fury often directed at her dad. On TV, Blake swallowed and let out a nervous laugh. "Well, at least we weren't on a roller coaster. I heard that one of them stopped upside down, right in the middle of a loop-de-loop!"

"Mom, Dad, I have to get to work." Zengo stood up and poured his hot chocolate into his to-go mug, screwing the cap on tight.

"But sweetheart, you barely touched your breakfast." Zengo's mother motioned to his spot at the table. She had his favorite cereal poured, and the toast was perfectly buttered.

Zengo kissed his mother on the cheek and grabbed the toast. "Thanks, Mom," he said. "Hate to eat and run, but duty calls."

As Zengo threw on his lucky leather jacket, he took one last glimpse of the news. Vanessa's face had been replaced by that of his favorite movie star. "Chase Mercy? What did he have to do with this?"

Max Pearson continued. "Just before opening the Kalamazoo City Dome last night, Mayor Saunders announced that filming is slated to begin there next week for the latest installment in the popular Spy Masterson film franchise, starring Kalamazoo City's native son and one of the world's biggest action stars, Chase Mercy. This marks Mercy's first return to the city in six years. Since last night's disaster, there

has been no comment from the mayor's office as to whether or not the movie shoot will begin as planned."

"Crazy!" said Zengo. He dashed to his car and threw it in gear. It wasn't even eight a.m., and this was already shaping up to be a pretty interesting day.

PLATYPUS POLICE SQUAD HEADQUARTERS, 7:40 A.M.

Zengo pushed his way past the night-shift officers who were checking out, and the day-shift officers who were checking in. As always, he took a quick moment to salute his grandfather's portrait, hanging in the lobby of the station. Then he stopped at the front desk to say hello to Peggy.

"Hey ya, Peggy, how are you this fine morning?" Zengo asked as she hung up her phone.

"Oh, hello . . . Detective Zengo . . . I'm fine . . . thank you." She managed a smile, even though she had clearly been on the job all night. But her smile fell as her phone rang again. "Excuse me, detective . . . another call. It's been a . . . busy morning."

"I bet. Have a good one, Peggy."

Zengo gave Peggy a nod, and hurried through the buzz and clamor of the busy squad room to where he and his partner's desks were.

"Detective Corey O'Malley?" Zengo's eyes widened in mock excitement. "*The* Detective Corey O'Malley? My friends are never going to believe this! Can I get your autograph?"

"Mornin', sport." O'Malley barely looked up from his computer.

Zengo, as usual, let the nickname slide. "Saw your daughter on the news this morning. Is she okay?" asked Zengo, setting his hot chocolate down at his desk. He fired up his own computer, adjusted his stapler so that it was perfectly parallel with the folders that were stacked by color, and gently brushed some of O'Malley's empty hot-dog cartons back over to his desk.

"Thanks for asking, kid. My little girl is a scrapper. Vanessa spent a few hours stuck on a ride, but she'll be fine. Not sure I can say the same for her relationship with her boyfriend," chuckled O'Malley.

"I'm sure that pleases you."

"Actually, that Blake kid was kinda growing on me." O'Malley swiveled his computer screen to show Zengo. It was filled with open windows, all showing archived articles from the *Kalamazoo City Krier* on the construction of the Dome. "Word is that what happened was a simple electrical malfunction, but if you ask me, there's too much riding on this Dome for us to take a disaster like this lightly."

"My thoughts exactly," said Zengo. "And I've got our first lead already. I hear that Maurice guy who ran the job is pretty shady."

O'Malley continued to open news files. "Perhaps. I'll say one thing for certain, though. Maurice Robertson is a savvy businessman. His firm beat out a lot of competition in the bid to build the mayor's little swamp playground."

Zengo walked around the desks to get a better look at O'Malley's screen. "So when do we get started? Has a case file been opened?"

"Not yet," said O'Malley.

Zengo looked toward Sergeant Plazinski's office. The door was shut, but the light was on. The sarge was in early, too. Their boss rarely closed his door unless he was reaming out his detectives, an experience Zengo and O'Malley were all too familiar with. But this morning there was barely a sound coming from the corner office—let alone the crash of a flying telephone.

"Vanessa told me that she saw something weird when she was stuck on top of the Ferris wheel last night," said O'Malley.

"So what are we waiting for? Let's check it out!"

"Shhhhhh." O'Malley leaned toward Zengo and whispered. "We're not the only ones jockeying for this case." O'Malley gave a quick glance and a nod across the room, where Detectives Diaz and Lucinni were yukking it up over by the watercooler.

Zengo followed O'Malley's glance. Their rivals looked like they were reenacting a lame comedy bit they must have seen on TV the night before, fart noises and all. But every few seconds they'd look over at Plazinski's door to see if he'd yet emerged.

"I hear you," said Zengo. "So, what did Vanessa see?"

"She snapped this photo with her phone when the blackout happened." O'Malley pulled up a blurry picture of the view of the water from the top of the sKCy Scraper. Zengo studied it. There wasn't much to see—just a flicker of light. He looked back at O'Malley, who  seemed to get what he was thinking, and nodded.

"I know: not much to go on. But she thought it could be something. Or more specifically—someone."

Zengo started to skim through the articles O'Malley had pulled up. "This is interesting," he said, pointing to one.

"What's that?" said O'Malley.

"None of the people the mayor hired for this project are from Kalamazoo City. You would think he would have gone out of his way to load the team up with locals—hometown pride and all. But all three of the Dome project leaders—the head of tourism, the architect, and the engineer who runs the company who constructed the Dome—are from out of town. No one even knows who they are. My dad found out that Maurice Robertson's company in Walhalla did the construction. He's always been Dad's biggest rival."

"I heard they weren't even planning to sell Frank's Franks at the Dome," said O'Malley. "That just tangles up my tail. If this tourism guru went along with building a dome that doesn't sell KC's best hot dogs, they don't know anything *about* this town."

A bad taste rose in Zengo's mouth, just as it did every time his partner mentioned his favorite hot-dog stand, which wasn't much more than some pieces of plywood stuck together by three generations of sausage grease. He decided to change the subject.

"Speaking of local talent, did you hear that Chase Mercy is going to be filming a movie at the Dome? Man, I've been watching his movies since I was a platypup. We all used to buy tickets for whatever kids' movie was playing, and then sneak in to see the latest Spy Masterson flick!"

O'Malley did not seem impressed. "*Hmphh.* I don't see what's so special about him. I went to high school with the guy, and knew him long before he went by the name Chase Mercy."

"Wait. That's not his real name?" Zengo's legions of action figures, piles of posters, and stacks of DVDs flashed across his mind, all of them emblazoned with the name Chase Mercy. Could this be true? "What is it, then?"

Before O'Malley could respond, Plazinski's door flew open. The sound of the door hitting the wall made everybody in the office jump—even Peggy, though she jumped a few seconds after everyone else.

"O'Malley! Zengo! Diaz! Lucinni!" Plazinski bellowed. "In my office, now!"

O'Malley was already standing and buttoning his sports coat. Zengo would have to wait for the inside scoop on Chase Mercy.

SERGEANT PLAZINSKI'S OFFICE, 8:00 A.M.

Plazinski motioned for his detectives to sit. The four platypuses did as they were told, huddling on the uncomfortable orange plastic chairs around Plazinski's desk. The sergeant sat down in his own chair, rolled up his sleeves, and brushed the sweat off his brow.

"Well, my friends, we have a heck of a situation on our hands. I've spoken to the mayor's office. They have assured me that the disaster at the Kalamazoo City Dome last night was nothing but a simple series of opening-day snafus."

"And you believe them?" Zengo asked.

"That's the official story. But the public won't feel safe until they have some real answers on what went down." Plazinski played with a pen on his desk. "O'Malley, I saw your daughter on the news this morning. I assume she's okay?"

O'Malley sat up in his chair. "Yes, she is. Thank you, sir."

"I read her statement. She saw something odd, didn't she?"

Zengo was impressed. The sarge had already read the pile of paperwork on Peggy's desk. What time had he gotten to work that morning?

"Well, sort of," said O'Malley. "While she was stuck at the top of the sKCy Scraper, she caught a glimpse of what looked like a small boat departing at the northeast corner of the Dome."

"Interesting. That's near where the fireworks display was housed." Plazinski glanced out the window. "We're lucky no lives were lost." He reached into his drawer and slapped some papers on his desk. "I've already requisitioned some search warrants. I want you four to head down to the Dome and see if there are any signs of foul play. I advised the mayor to close the

Dome for a bit, but he won't give us very much time. He wants to reopen as soon as possible. Our city needs the Dome to be a success. And never mind ticket sales— if it's not perceived to be safe, Chase Mercy and his film crew won't be coming to town."

"Why would someone want to jeopardize the film shoot?" Diaz asked.

"Maybe somebody from Walhalla?" Zengo offered immediately.

"What?" Plazinski barked. "Rookie, you going to tell us where that theory is coming from?"

Rookie again. It was as if his theories didn't even matter. "Sir, the engineer who built the dome is from Walhalla. The tourism guru is from Walhalla. And the contractor? He isn't from Kalamazoo City, either."

"An interesting set of coincidences, I suppose," said Plazinski. "But coincidences don't prove anything. Sure, we've got a long-standing rivalry with

Walhalla. But our two towns settle their differences on the baseball field. Before anyone accuses folks from Walhalla of plotting against our fair city to the tune of putting lives in danger, I want to see some concrete leads. Put your bills to the ground and sweep your tails around that Dome. All of you. Now, go! Get out of my office ten minutes ago!"

Diaz and Lucinni pounded fists and made for the door. But as O'Malley left their boss's office, Plazinski stopped him. Zengo hung back too.

"Hey, even though your kid was there last night, don't let any of this get personal."

"I won't, Sarge."

Plazinski looked at Zengo, and he nodded as well. "All right, get moving."

THE KALAMAZOO CITY DOME, 9:20 A.M.

"Sorry, we're not open yet." The security guard's voice crackled over the speaker on the front gate. O'Malley was not amused.

He pressed the buzzer again, and held up his badge and the warrant to the security camera. "Platypus Police Squad. We have a warrant. Open this dang gate!"

The gate swung open and Zengo entered with O'Malley by his side, and Diaz and Lucinni just behind.

Zengo was instantly awestruck. The place was unbelievable. He had never seen so many different rides, and such incredibly cool ones. Whether everything behind the scenes and under the hood was up to snuff, he had no idea. But he had to admit the first impression was pretty impressive.

Even so, it was eerie to be in this vast building with just the other three detectives—especially given what had gone down the night before. If Zengo had not had an early a.m. shift, he probably would have been one of the first in line on opening night. Of course, if he been there, he would definitely have been able to keep everyone calm. Zengo imagined himself leading everyone to safety as if he were in a Chase Mercy movie himself.

O'Malley didn't waste any time.

"All right, guys, Zengo and I will scope out the main grounds. Diaz, Lucinni—you guys go check the administration offices on the west side of the park. See if you can chat up any security guards."

"Hey, Diaz, look, it's Mayor Saunders himself," scoffed Lucinni. "What gives you the right to hand out these orders, O'Malley?"

Diaz snickered and opened his bill to add to the ribbing, but before he could, O'Malley turned on them with a glare so fierce that it stopped them dead in their tracks, even though he was about a foot shorter than either of them.

"Get to gettin', Detectives," he said.

"All right, all right. Come on, Diaz." Lucinni grabbed

his partner by the arm and they waddled off.

Zengo liked seeing his partner throw his weight around—especially since the anger was not directed at him. He and O'Malley walked down the Dome's main street, a bright-green stripe painted down the center of the complex. Smaller avenues shot off from each side, leading to a wealth of attractions.

Kiddy Land, a section for the youngest of Kalamazooians, was painted with vibrant colors. Zengo thought that it would have been the end-all of awesomeness if you were a kid. A ride labeled THE LADYBUG swirled little ladybuglike cars around in circles. Another, called the Whaler, was a miniature boat ride where the passengers were sprayed by an animatronic whale. Zengo thought he would have most enjoyed the Mosquito, a miniature roller coaster that

couldn't have been eight feet off the ground. Adjacent to the kid-centric section was a giant arcade that was filled with both the newest video games for the younger kids, but also some vintage eight-bit cabinets for the older gamers. Zengo felt the quarters burning holes in his pocket, and his thumbs twitched, but he knew now was not the time to get his game on, even if he could easily throw his initials up on Quack-Man's high-score board.

Everywhere you looked, there was some sort of ride or concession stand. A person could drop fifty bucks in less than twenty minutes. No wonder the mayor promised increased revenues for the city. It was still early in the morning, but Zengo salivated at the thought of how delicious the fried cupcakes must taste.

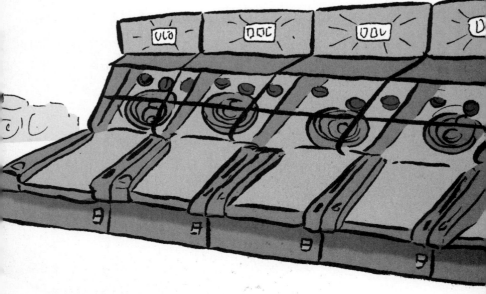

"This really would be the perfect setting for a Chase Mercy movie." Zengo imagined the action star jumping off of the roller-coaster tracks, doing backflips, and chucking boomerangs at the bad guys.

O'Malley rolled his eyes. At least Zengo figured that was what he was doing behind those sunglasses of his. "You mean Chadwick Mickleheimer."

"You're serious?" said Zengo. "*Chadwick Mickleheimer?* Really? You said you knew him in high school?"

"Oh yeah. His older brother was my best friend. He and I were both on the Kal East football team back in the day."

"Was Chase on the team too?"

"Nope. His brother, Andrew, was a great guy and a great teammate, but Chadwick, to be honest . . ." O'Malley shook his head. "Let's just say he wasn't built for football. Or for anything else, really. He usually just kept to himself, always refused to hang out with Drew and me. Everyone called him Squirt, if I remember right."

Zengo couldn't believe what he was hearing, but at that moment something else caught his attention. "Hey, look!"

They had come to a sign that pointed to an attraction called the "Kalamazoo City River of Dreams." A miniature replica of the Kalamazoo City skyline rose up before them—it was all there, every detail of the city they loved, meticulously recreated. In all of the

chaos last night, somebody had forgotten to turn the ride off. Boats turned the corner of a man-made river and ran along a track that disappeared into a small opening underneath a miniature of Pandini Tower.

"Want to take a spin?" said Zengo. "You know, look for clues?"

"Hmm. Not sure if you're old enough to ride, slugger," chuckled O'Malley.

"Actually, you need to be this tall to ride," quipped Zengo as he pointed to the height requirement next to the ride, only a few inches below O'Malley's head. "On your tiptoes, you just make it. Come on, let's jump into one of these boats."

"I was actually saving all of my fingerprint dust for the horsies over on the merry-go-round," sneered O'Malley.

"Aw, come on, partner," said Zengo. "Plazinski wants us to leave no stone unturned."

"You go ahead, kid," said O'Malley. "I want to inspect the Ferris wheel."

"Suit yourself," Zengo said. Then he called over his shoulder. "Remember what the sergeant said—don't let this get personal."

O'Malley took off his sunglasses. "That little piece of wisdom goes for us both, partner." Zengo followed O'Malley's eyes to a line written on the sign beneath the ride's title: PAID FOR BY THE GENEROUS SUPPORT OF PANDINI ENTERPRISES. "You go ahead and jump on one of those boats—that is, if you can deal with those raging rapids. I'm going to move along on foot."

O'Malley left before Zengo could come up with a halfway decent comeback to O'Malley's jab about Zengo's permanent suspicion of Frank Pandini Jr.— and his fear of water.

Zengo jumped aboard a tiny blue boat as it turned the corner, bumping his knees up against the safety guard as he did. He was carried into the ride. The temperature dropped about twenty degrees. The junior detective was enveloped in pure darkness as he floated past the entrance. Sounds of dinosaurs filtered in from either side, followed by a large explosion. Then a sliver of light illuminated a caveplatypus grunting atop a rock formation. The animatronic looked so lifelike, Zengo thought the figure banging rocks together would suddenly turn and look at him. The Neanderthal worked furiously, banging rocks on top of a pile of fallen tree branches. Soon a spark flickered and the pile turned into a flame. Orchestral music dramatically filled the room, and a deep, gravelly voice began to narrate. "Welcome to the Kalamazoo City River of Dreams. On this voyage, you will witness the marvels that this city has brought the world. It is home to many inventions that have helped define civilization, including the invention of fire."

Zengo hardly believed *that* was true. But the voice sounded so confident and . . . familiar. Zengo listened

"From the dawn of time to the days of the early settlers, this land was rich with resources. Even the visionary pioneers who founded what we now call Kalamazoo City could never have imagined the boundless riches that this fine city would cultivate. Sir Calvin Kalamazoo claimed this territory as his own and constructed the first few buildings. Many followed Sir Kalamazoo's lead, and soon our beautiful town began to grow."

He finally recognized the voice—it was Chase Mercy.

Zengo sailed past a menagerie of early settlers constructing homes, building churches, and engineering bridges. "During the industrial revolution, the citizens of Kalamazoo City embraced the changing times and shifted their industry from farming to manufacturing."

As his boat chugged along, a roomful of similarly dressed animals worked on machines to create wind-up toys. "Yes, the windup toy, a cheery distraction for youth worldwide, was invented here in Kalamazoo City!"

Looming ahead was what looked like a skeleton of the Kalamazoo City skyline. "In the early 1900s, the population of Kalamazoo City grew exponentially. No longer did the citizens look outward to settle, but upward! Skyscrapers were all the rage, and we were among the first in the country to build these magnificent structures. All the entrepreneurs in town, along with their architects of choice, raced to outdo one another—in both style and altitude.

"Of course, Kalamazoo City has had its dark days. Frank Pandini, one of the most nefarious crime lords in the nation's history, made his home right here in

Kalamazoo." Zengo's fur stood on end as he examined the animatronic Frank Pandini. The family resemblance between him and his son, billionaire and man-about-town Frank Pandini Jr., was uncanny. Zengo remembered with mixed feelings his first case as a Platypus Police Squad detective, when he had suspected Frank Jr. of being behind a string of illegal fish deals. Though he was cleared of all charges, Zengo still didn't completely trust him.

Chase Mercy's voice continued. "Mr. Frank Pandini's ring of crime terrorized the city until he was taken down by Lieutenant Andrew Dailey of the Platypus Police Squad."

Zengo's eyes welled up. His breath caught. The robotic statue of his dearly departed grandfather was so realistic that Zengo wanted to jump out of the boat to visit with him. Over the music, his grandfather began to speak about his quest to protect the city and leave it a better place than he found it. But something was wrong. The movement of his grandfather's bill didn't match the sound playing from the speakers. It made his grandpa seem like nothing more than a cheesy attraction.

The voice of Chase Mercy cut through the family reunion. "Dailey's hard work and bravery sent Pandini to prison, but that didn't save the brave platypus from the mob boss's claws. The corrupt king-pin lived out his remaining days behind bars, but he still ran Kalamazoo City with a thirst for vengeance and fury. Tragically, Lieutenant Dailey was taken out while on a routine inspection of downtown businesses. While Frank Pandini Sr. was undoubtedly behind the murder, the actual culprits were never caught."

Tears welled up in Zengo's eyes, and he might have begun to cry if the little blue boat hadn't moved past this sad scene.

"Pandini's notorious legacy, however, has been atoned for by his son, Frank Pandini Jr., one of the most brilliant businessmen and generous philan-thropists the city has ever known. After making his fortunes through legitimate real-estate deals, Frank Jr. has returned to Kalamazoo City and constructed the crown jewel of the downtown skyline—Pandini Tower. Situated in the center of town, this sparkling edifice is one of the tallest and most impressive build-ings in the world."

The music shifted to a peppier tune as the boat turned a corner. "Kalamazoo is also the home of the planet's most daring action star—me, Chase Mercy!"

Zengo found himself face-to-face with a life-size Chase Mercy. Hands on his hips, a dangerous glint in his eye, the animatronic Chase wore his signature Spy Masterson tuxedo and looked as heroic as he ever had in his movies. But all Zengo could think about was *squirt*. That wasn't so different from *rookie*. He knew how Chase probably felt.

"A new era is upon us here in Kalamazoo City. During Mayor Saunders's tenure, the city has witnessed unparalleled growth, leading to the triumph that is the Kalamazoo City Dome, one of the nation's foremost tourist attractions. Kalamazoo may already have a long and distinguished history, but this is truly just the beginning."

The ride ended with a coronet fanfare. Zengo jumped off the boat as soon as it came to a stop, and grabbed his radio. He had an idea, and he wanted to run it by his partner right away.

"O'Malley, come in, O'Malley."

Zengo looked from left to right for any sign of his partner as his radio crackled to life.

"Yeah, rook. I'm here."

Zengo huffed over the rookie comment. He was really getting sick of this. "O'Malley, I just had a thought. Frank Pandini Jr. can't be too happy with how his father was depicted in this river ride, especially considering the fact that he paid for it. I think we should check out his alibi for last night, see if we can find his paw prints in the disaster."

"Sounds like you're letting your feet get ahead of your skis, kid," said O'Malley. "Remember the last time you accused him of a crime like this?"

"O'Malley, open your eyes! Can't you see his motivation here?"

"My eyes are open, kid. And they're looking at Mr. Pandini right now."

"Huh?"

"Yeah, kid, I've just had an interesting conversation with the man. I think you should come by the sKCy Scraper to hear what he has to say."

Zengo brought the radio closer to his bill and whispered, "He heard everything I just said, didn't he?"

"Every single word, rookie."

THE SKCY SCRAPER, 9:50 A.M.

Frank Pandini Jr. filed his claws as he accepted Zengo's babbled attempt at an explanation.

"There is no need to apologize," said Pandini as he placed the emery board back into his inner jacket pocket. "I appreciate your thoroughness, Detective."

"Mr. Pandini is here today to take a look around the grounds of the Dome," said O'Malley, in an obvious attempt to defuse the tension.

Zengo wondered how Pandini managed to get past the gates. Even the badge-carrying Platypus Police Squad had needed search warrants. But he supposed

41

all doors in this city were open to Pandini.

O'Malley continued, with a slight smile, "Mr. Chase Mercy Superfan, you will be happy to know that it was Mr. Pandini who brokered the deal to get the new film shot here in Kalamazoo City."

Pandini's typically composed exterior showed a small crack. "I worked incredibly hard and put a lot on the line to convince Worldwide Films to shoot on location here," he said. "And now the studio is threatening to shut down the whole operation and take production up to Walhalla if this Dome is deemed unsafe."

Zengo lifted an eyebrow. *Walhalla? Interesting.*

"No site in Walhalla can compare to the Dome for sheer scale," said O'Malley.

"True, but they have the MegaMall," said Pandini. "The screenwriters are already rewriting the script, should the Dome prove unsuitable."

Zengo knew Walhalla's MegaMall all too well. That was where he went on his one and only visit to Walhalla. He had been a teenager. The kids who hung out at the MegaMall treated him like scum for being from Kalamazoo City. One of those punks had even knocked the slushie right out of his hand. Zengo had vowed never to go back there.

"That's not good," said O'Malley.

"No, not at all," said Pandini. "There's a lot of dough on the line. A major motion picture brings in a huge revenue boost to a city. Everybody from the actors to the cameramen to the prop masters will need a place to stay—our hotels will be full. And they all need to eat—our restaurants will thrive."

Sure. Your *hotels and* your *restaurants will thrive,* Zengo thought.

"Which is why I wanted to come down here personally to see what was going on," Pandini continued, hitching his shoulders and tugging down the sleeves of his tuxedo jacket. "I'm not used to a business with which I'm involved opening to such disastrous returns. But then, this project is Mayor Saunders's, not mine."

The sKCy Scraper suddenly creaked to life and began to spin around.

"Whoa!" said Zengo. "Looks like Mayor Saunders decided to open up shop today after all."

"A good businessman—or public official, for that matter—knows he needs to get his ducks in a row before he opens a major public facility," said Pandini, looking around. "Unfortunately, there is nary a duck in sight."

Zengo surveyed the scene. Pandini was right. No one had shown up for the Dome's second day in business, duck or otherwise. At least, not yet. But who would want to go on any of these rides when they could break down at any moment?

Pandini's phone rang. He reached into the interior breast pocket of his tuxedo jacket and answered. "Carpy, speak to me. Uh-huh. Right." Pandini looked to both detectives as he spoke. "I'll be right there." Pandini hung up and put the phone away. "Sorry about that. Problem down at my nightclub. Listen, please do call on me if you need anything. You're always welcome at any of my establishments. You know I take care of those who take care of this fine city of ours."

O'Malley and Zengo watched Pandini stalk away. When he was fully out of earshot, O'Malley laid into Zengo. "Are you satisfied now? Or am I going to spend the rest of *this* case listening to your Pandini conspiracy theories, just like last time?"

"No, you've got me there," Zengo conceded. "That man loves one thing, and that's money. He needs the Dome to be a success just as much as the mayor does—maybe even more so."

O'Malley glanced at his watch. "C'mon, let's go find Diaz and Lucinni and see if they've come up with anything. Because you and me? We've got nothin'."

"Sure, hold up one sec, though." Zengo had noticed that the carnival game stations were now open. He moseyed up to one and slapped down a five-dollar bill. The carny working the game station handed over three baseballs in return.

"Knock down the bottles, yah get a prize of yah choice," he said, gesturing to the rows of knockoff cartoon plushies.

Zengo focused on the bottles, stacked in a pyramid. He whipped the first ball, and hit them dead-on. But the bottles didn't budge. O'Malley took off his sunglasses. Zengo considered the second ball in his hand, chucked it at the pyramid, and made a direct hit. Again, nothing.

"What gives?!" Zengo asked.

"Just gotta throw the balls hardah, my friend," the carny said, leaning back in his chair, barely paying attention.

Zengo gripped the third ball in his hand, and whipped it with all of his might. Again, he hit the bottles, but they didn't fall.

"C'mon, son," said O'Malley as he grabbed his partner's arm. "This nonsense isn't worth our time."

"I know a scam when I see one," said Zengo.

The four detectives met back up at the front gate. Diaz and Lucinni had succumbed to the concession stands. Lucinni was furiously trying to lick ice cream that was dripping down the side of a waffle cone, while Diaz munched on cotton candy.

"That security team is nothing but a bunch of hired thugs," Diaz grumbled as they crossed the parking lot to return to their cars. "They are about as dysfunctional as the rides they were hired to protect." He looked around for a napkin, his claws covered in congealed sugar.

"They don't even archive their surveillance footage," Lucinni added. "What in the hay is the point of having cameras planted around the park?"

O'Malley shook his head. "That doesn't make any sense," he said. "The mayor is always threatening our budget, and yet he doesn't bring in the Platypus

Police Squad to run security for his little pet project. He hires these subpar rent-a-cops."

"You get what you pay for," said Lucinni.

"Sure do," added Diaz. "Especially considering that we found something they didn't even spot."

Zengo and O'Malley followed Diaz and Lucinni over to a small, gray shed with a door marked ELECTRICAL CONTROL STATION. Inside, it was easy to see what likely caused the blackout.

"All the fuses under the control panel here have been bashed to bits," said Lucinni. "And it appears like whoever did it used this." He showed them a scarred and battered wrench casually discarded in the corner of the room.

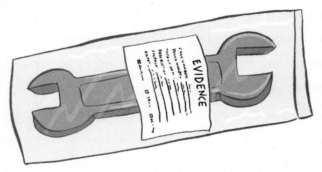

O'Malley pulled out gloves and an evidence bag, and collected the wrench. "Looks like we've got ourselves some foul play, boys. I suppose any security footage of people coming in and out of this room last night wasn't archived?"

Diaz shook his head. "Too bad Frank Pandini Jr. isn't running the place. We'd have five different camera angles on whoever did this."

"Speaking of which," said O'Malley as they walked back to the front gate, "we just saw Mr. Pandini here at the park."

"Oh, is that right?" Diaz snickered. "Zengo, did you try and tackle him?"

Zengo was in no mood for getting ribbed by those fools. He was still a little emotional after meeting up with his animatronic grandpa. And he was more than a little heated about being cheated by the carny. He hitched his shoulders and walked ahead silently.

"Let the kid be," O'Malley said to Diaz and Lucinni as he opened his car door. Just then, the radio crackled to life. "Car one-fifty-three, come in." It was Sergeant Plazinski. Zengo reached for the receiver, but O'Malley snatched it first.

"Ten-four, sir. O'Malley here." Diaz and Lucinni shared a sideways look. Zengo was psyched that Plazinski had called *their* car, not the chuckleheads'.

"What did you uncover down at the Dome?"

"It appears someone purposely destroyed the fuses in the electrical control station, which is presumably what caused the blackout. It appears we might have a crime on our hands, Sarge. Unfortunately, because it was amateur night in the security office, we don't have any footage of anyone entering and exiting the control station. But we did collect a wrench that the perpetrator likely used on the fuses, which I want to bring in for fingerprinting."

"Interesting," said Plazinski. "Okay, given these developments, I want you and Zengo to go talk to Derek Dougherty. His photographs are all over the paper—apparently he was on the scene last night. He might have a shot of your saboteur."

"Yes, sir. What about Diaz and Lucinni?"

"Send them back to the station with the wrench for the lab. I want them to sort through the paperwork that's come in since last night."

"Well, you heard the man," said O'Malley as he tossed the evidence bag to Diaz and Lucinni. Lucinni dropped his cone and caught the wrench. Zengo wondered what was more disappointing to the oaf— paperwork, or the ice cream that was splattered across the pavement. Lucinni hopped into the car next to his partner, turned the key in the ignition, and they were off in a cloud of exhaust.

O'Malley and Zengo jumped into their squad car, pounded fists, then sped off in the other direction.

KALAMAZOO CITY KRIER CENTRAL OFFICES, 11:10 A.M.

Zengo stepped out of the squad car, slamming the door behind him. He looked up at the *Kalamazoo City Krier*'s iconic logo looming over the ornate front doors of the newspaper's headquarters. He grinned at his partner.

"Never thought you'd be knockin' on Dougherty's door, did you?" he said.

"Hmmph," replied O'Malley as he straightened out his sports coat and fastened its buttons.

"He does have a good eye; you have to give him

that," said Zengo, holding up the day's newspaper. Derek's photo of frenzied carnival-goers filled the top half of the front page, beneath the headline DISASTER AT THE DOME.

"Yeah, yeah," O'Malley grumbled. "What gets me is, every time I turn around, he's poking his snout into our business."

"How about if we try to stay on his good side at least long enough to get a look at the photos that didn't make it into the paper?" said Zengo. He was so hungry for evidence his stomach was rumbling. Or maybe he was just plain hungry.

"We'll see," said O'Malley.

The detectives pushed open the front doors and stepped into the reception area. Awards filled the walls, going way back into the last century. *Classy operation,* thought Zengo, proud of his hometown paper.

"How may I help you?" mumbled the reception-ist without looking up from her magazine. She was reading a copy of *Wow!,* which surprised Zengo. Why read a gossip rag when you could get a free copy of the *Krier* every day? Then he noticed who graced the cover—Chase Mercy. The headline read MERCY ME! WHO IS CHASE DATING THIS WEEK?

54

Before either detective could respond, a familiar voice rang out. "Well, well, well, Detectives! Were you looking for me or should I direct you to the crossword department?" Derek Dougherty swished his tail and smiled at his own wisecrack.

"How did he know we were coming?" muttered O'Malley. "That runt must have eyes in the back of his head."

Derek smirked and said, "I always monitor the police scanners, so I figured you two were on your way here. Plazinski wants to know more about what went down last night, right? I took a load of pictures. Come on."

Zengo and O'Malley followed Derek through a maze of cubicles. In spite of his partner's attitude, Zengo admired the feisty little reporter. He had moxie. Plus, he always seemed to be in the right place at the right time.

Derek's cubicle was a spectacular mess. Stacks of old newspapers teetered in dangerous piles. Camera equipment was heaped in a corner. The walls were covered with layers of photos, all stabbed

with thumbtacks. Every other available surface was crowded with used takeout cartons. The overall effect was chaos, and the overall odor was . . . interesting.

"Please, have a seat." Derek gestured loosely, as if there were somewhere to actually sit.

The two detectives remained standing.

"Let's just cut to the chase, Derek," said O'Malley. "No time to lollygag. Get those photos out. NOW."

Derek picked his teeth with a letter opener and showed no sign of standing up. "I'm sure they're around here somewhere. . . ."

O'Malley tensed up, and Zengo got ready to yank his partner back by the tail. O'Malley was ordinarily a levelheaded dude, but this Dougherty character knew how to slither right under the old man's fur.

"Listen up, snoop," growled O'Malley. "You were at the Dome last night when things went haywire. You got some shots. We'd like to see them. Don't make me repeat myself."

Derek stared intently into O'Malley's eyes, not budging. "Why should I show them to you?" he said. "Why don't you just ask the Dome security guards? I'm sure they got everything there was to see."

"You're kidding, right?" said Zengo. "Those clowns?"

Derek pulled out his notepad. "May I quote you on that?" he said, scribbling.

"What? No!" said O'Malley. "Are you going to help us? Or are we going to have to come back with a warrant?"

Maybe O'Malley's outrage was actually getting to the brash little reporter. Or maybe he was tired of playing cat-and-mouse. Derek opened his desk drawer, saying, "All right already, keep your socks on." He snatched a stack of photographs and offered them to the detectives. O'Malley grabbed them and handed half to Zengo, saying, "Let's get to looking."

Zengo took his pile of pictures and flipped through them. He didn't see anything unusual at first—a cotton-candy machine, a booth full of the type of cheap and cheery stuff people win at carnivals and then throw away, crowds of people waiting in lines. He stopped to study a photograph of the ScreamerCoaster more closely.

"Looks like fun," he said.

"You couldn't pay me enough money to ride that thing," Derek scoffed.

"Afraid of heights?" Zengo asked.

"No, I'm afraid of poorly constructed rides," Derek replied. "That's the coaster that stopped for two hours upside down when the Dome broke down."

Zengo put down his stack of photographs. "What do you know about the team behind the construction of the Dome, Derek?"

"You mean the mayor's Dream Team?" said Derek with a sneer. "Saunders talked about it like he had made the deal of the century for the city. But if you ask me, I think it's Saunders who's getting the best of this deal, taking money for himself."

"What makes you say that?" Zengo asked. O'Malley stopped rifling through his pile of photos and looked up.

"Let's see . . ." said Derek. "He made no-bid sweet-heart deals with contractors from out of town; he dodged tax codes; he pushed his own agenda through city council to build this thing. The whole situation stinks."

Zengo couldn't help but agree, but wondered if Dougherty would still pick up such an odor if he took his trash out from time to time.

"I think the guy has something to gain from

this—beyond the glory of his legacy," Derek continued. "And I'm going to get to the bottom of it!"

"That's quite the accusation," O'Malley said.

"It's a free country. I can say whatever I want." Derek
leaned back against the wall of his cubicle. "Obviously
I won't print anything until I have proof. I've tried to
get interviews with the members of the Dream Team,
but I've been completely shut out. Something ain't
right at City Hall. And Corey, you of all people should
know what I mean."

"It's *Detective O'Malley* to you," snapped the senior
detective.

Derek shrugged, indifferent to O'Malley's blus-
ter. "What*ever.* All I'm saying is, this whole situation
makes me dizzier than a busted Tilt-A-Whirl."

As O'Malley and Derek sparred, Zengo kept flipping
through the photos. He stopped to study a picture of
the ribbon-cutting ceremony. The mayor was flanked
by three smiling faces. They had to be Audrey
Davis, Maurice Robertson, and Frederick Treeger.
The Dream Team. Zengo narrowed his eyes. Why
had the mayor brought these three characters on
board? What was their connection? His brain began
to churn.

"Derek, would you mind if we kept a few of these photos?" he asked.

"Knock yourself out, Detective. I can print more."

"What do you have there?" O'Malley asked.

"I'm curious about this Dream Team." Zengo held up the photo to his partner. "They're all a bit of a mystery, and I have a feeling we're looking at our culprit in one of those three."

"Let's not jump to any conclusions, kid," O'Malley huffed as he continued to flip through photographs. Zengo was used to the O'Malley brush-off. He and his partner often reached the same conclusions from different directions.

Zengo noticed O'Malley's eyebrows lift. "What is it?" he asked. He stood up to look over his partner's shoulder. In O'Malley's hands were scenes from the blackout.

"My infrared lens captures pictures in the dark," bragged Derek.

The photographs were terrifying. People clung to

malfunctioning rides, their faces frozen in horror. Throngs of people desperately shoved one another aside, trying to get to the exits. There was even a photo of a heartbroken girl who had dropped her fried cupcake on the ground. *Man, that looked tasty,* thought Zengo. Each picture offered clues as to what took place in the disaster. But what—or who—had caused it?

O'Malley and Zengo pored over all the pictures, hoping for any sort of lead. Then they found one. It was a photo of a small figure who appeared to be running. The photo was too blurry to see the person clearly. The only thing they could see was that in one hand, the figure carried a wrench. From the looks of it, it was the same one they had found in the amusement park by the busted fuse box.

The detectives shared a silent glance. Derek leaned forward to peer at the photo, but O'Malley quickly buried it among the stack.

"We'll be taking all of these photographs back to the station," O'Malley said.

"At least let me see the ones you're interested in," said Derek, reaching his hand out to grab for the photos. O'Malley intercepted his hand and shook it firmly.

"Derek, you have been an invaluable asset to this investigation, and I thank you for fulfilling your civic duty."

Taking O'Malley's lead, Zengo scooped up the remaining photographs and navigated out through the maze of cubicles.

PLATYPUS POLICE SQUAD HEADQUARTERS, 12:30 P.M.

The confiscated photographs hung on the evidence wall as O'Malley and Zengo ate their lunches and attempted to piece together the events of the Dome blackout. Zengo watched O'Malley take a bite out of his chili dog. As expected, chili sauce dripped out of the bun and down O'Malley's tie before coming to rest on his shirtfront.

Zengo heard a mail cart's squeaky wheel, and turned around to greet the office secretary.

"Good . . . afternoon . . . Detectives. Do you have . . .

any mail . . . to go out?"

"Hey there, Peggy," said O'Malley. "No mail here, but thanks for asking."

The old turtle looked up at the evidence wall. "What have . . . we got . . . here?"

"Photos from last night's Dome Disaster," said Zengo as he pulled down the one and only photo that had a glimpse of the culprit. "We think we found a suspect in this picture, but it's blurry. There isn't enough information here to make any sort of ID."

"Hmmm," said Peggy as she put on her glasses and peered closely at the picture. "May I . . . borrow this?" Zengo looked to O'Malley. What could she possibly do with this picture? Make a macaroni frame for it? What if she lost it? Zengo was about to say *no thanks* when O'Malley piped up.

"Sure thing, Peggy. But please bring it right back."

"Will . . . do. In . . . a . . . jiffy."

The sound of the receding squeaky wheels were drowned out by the yelling that suddenly erupted from Plazinski's office. Somebody was getting reamed in there.

Zengo and O'Malley quickly moved to their favorite eavesdropping spot. Both detectives were surprised to see Diaz and Lucinni were already there.

"Huh. I thought for sure it was you guys in there," snarled O'Malley.

"And we thought it was you two clowns," cracked Diaz.

"Nice shirt, Corey," giggled Lucinni, gesturing to a stain. "Saving a snack for later?"

"Who's in there?" Zengo whispered as he stepped closer to the door.

"Don't know," said Lucinni.

The shouting stopped abruptly. The detectives heard footsteps coming toward the door. All four platypuses shuffled to get out of the way, stumbling over one another's tails as they did. The door flew open and crashed against the wall.

Out stepped Plazinski. Zengo noticed the familiar anger vein pulsing in his superior's forehead. He hadn't been the one yelling—he was the one getting yelled at. By someone with talons. And a sharp suit. Who had been elected mayor more than any politician in the history of Kalamazoo City.

Mayor Saunders stepped out of Plazinski's office, ducking his head to avoid the doorframe. He nodded toward the detectives, who were trying to look

casual, and failing miserably. "Detectives," he said, straightening out his jacket. He turned to Plazinski and extended his feathered wing for a shake. "Good day, Sergeant. I know I can count on you."

Plazinski extended his webbed hand and gripped Saunders's wing firmly. "You can. I will protect and serve the good people of this city."

By the look on Saunders's face, that wasn't the answer he was looking for. What more could a mayor want, wondered Zengo.

The detective squad stood frozen as Mayor Saunders walked past Processing toward Peggy's desk. The suave politician smiled and shook hands with everyone he passed. When the mayor was out of sight, the detectives were all still staring at their feet. You could cut the tension with a machete. They all knew better than to say anything.

When the mayor left the building, Plazinski broke the silence. "That good-for-nothin' politician. They're all the same." Zengo was taken aback. In his short time on the force, he had already learned one thing: Plazinski was nearly always on the side of the powers-that-be.

Now Zengo was dying of curiosity. He wished someone would at least ask Plazinski what was going on. He glanced at the others, his eyes begging them to take the lead. But everyone else kept their traps shut. Finally he couldn't stand it any longer. "What was that all about?"

"Apparently Mayor Saunders isn't happy with the

fact that I sent you guys down to his playground today," Plazinski snarled. "He wants us to step back and let him sort out the disaster at the Dome."

"So we're off the case?" asked Diaz.

"Do I look like the kind of sergeant who would close down this case because some ostrich got his feathers ruffled?" screamed Plazinski, his bill shoved right in Diaz's. "If anybody in this department thinks I'm just going to roll over and lay an egg because the mayor tells me to, well, then I'd be happy to pass out a stack of tickets and send him out to check for expired parking meters. No, I'm going to turn up the heat on this thing."

Zengo wondered if he should tell the sarge about the photo they found. He glanced at O'Malley, whose face was unreadable. "Sergeant, you might want to know about something that O'Malley and I noticed in the photographs we confiscated from the *Kalamazoo City Krier.*"

"What is it, kid?" asked Plazinski, glaring at Zengo as he took a step toward him.

"Um, well. It isn't much, sir. We found one photo with the wrench that may have been used in damaging the electrical unit at the Dome, but the photo is blurry."

"*Was* . . . blurry," said Peggy as she handed Zengo the original photograph and a printout of a digitally enhanced version of the picture. "I guess . . . they . . . didn't tell . . . you, Ricky. I'm pretty good . . . with forensic digital . . . imaging. Everything . . . was right . . . there. Right in . . . the photo."

"Peggy, this is incredible!" Zengo grabbed the picture with a grateful smile. The figure in the photo was tiny. The wrench was nearly as big as he was. And he had a big chunk taken out of one ear. It looked like it had been bitten off.

O'Malley was looking over his shoulder. "That's the same wrench we recovered from the electrical station. And look at the guy holding it. He's wearing a Kalamazoo Dome security uniform!"

"So maybe the wrench really did belong to him," said Zengo. "As someone who works at the Dome, he could have a legit reason to be carrying around tools. Could someone else have stolen it from him to bash in the electrical system?"

"Nope," said Diaz. "There was only one set of prints on the wrench. I think we're looking at our perp here."

This might be the break they were looking for. "No wonder he could sneak around restricted areas during the opening-night festivities," said Zengo. "He didn't have to worry about security. He *was* security!"

Plazinski took the evidence in hand and barked, "Diaz, Lucinni, I want all of the employee records that you recovered from the Dome on my desk immediately!"

Diaz and Lucinni each shuffled their weight and fidgeted with their badges.

"What's the matter? Get a move on, boys!" barked Plazinski.

"Um . . . here's the thing . . ." began Diaz.

"Yeah, about those files . . ." continued Lucinni.

Plazinski's forehead vein had popped out again. This wasn't going to be pretty. "Do *not* tell me that you went all the way to the Dome with a search warrant and you didn't bring back info on one single employee there?"

"Uh. No. No, we didn't," said Lucinni, looking at his webbed feet.

"Diaz! Lucinni! New Berry Street! Get a supply of parking tickets from Peggy. That's your beat until further notice."

Ouch, thought Zengo. Plazinski had banished Diaz and Lucinni to the snooty shopping district on the north side of town. It was a weekday. They would be dealing with rich people who didn't take kindly to officers telling them where they could and couldn't park. That was a lousy assignment.

"WHAT ARE YOU WAITING FOR?" Plazinski screamed. "GET OUT OF MY SIGHT BEFORE I START THROWING THINGS!" Diaz and Lucinni stumbled off. The sergeant turned to his two remaining detectives. "Well, boys, looks like this case is yours. I want you to find out everything you can about the fellow in this picture. And do so without anybody knowing you're sniffing around his tail, understand? If word gets out that we're looking for someone who works at the Dome, we're going to have a real angry mayor on our hands."

"We're all over it, Sarge," said O'Malley, snapping to attention. He was about to say more, but Plazinski had already slammed his office door shut so hard that the photo of him shaking hands with the governor fell off the wall.

THE KALAMAZOO CITY DOME SECURITY OFFICE, 1:35 P.M.

"Sorry, files are classified," said the officer on duty at the Dome, bits of tuna flying out of his mouth as he talked. The plump guard was flanked by television screens showing the feeds from security cameras positioned throughout the Dome. His uniform wasn't clean, and it barely fit. His badge wasn't even pinned on straight. O'Malley could be a mess at times, but nothing like this.

"Let me repeat myself," said O'Malley calmly. "We're going to need to see files on all of the Dome's security employees."

"Let *me* repeat *myself*: they're confidential," he said, wiping his mouth.

Who does this guy think he is? thought Zengo.

"All right, then," said O'Malley after a moment. "You have yourself a great day."

Zengo whispered, "What are you doing?"

"Shut your bill, kid." O'Malley grabbed Zengo's arm as he turned to leave. Then he stopped in the doorway and turned to the possum. "Oh, before we go, do you have a bathroom around here? One too many of those delicious Dome slushies."

"You can go 'head and use the staff bathroom just down the hall." The possum gestured to where the detectives could find the restrooms. Zengo knew O'Malley was up to something, but what clues did he hope to find in the bathroom? Would the toilet paper lead them to the answers they needed?

"Thank you, sir. I apologize for the inconvenience."

O'Malley led Zengo to the bathroom. "What the heck was that?!" Zengo whispered. "Why are we in here rather than out there, giving that rent-a-cop the third degree? He probably won that badge at one of the prize booths!"

O'Malley swung open the bathroom door and

pushed Zengo in. Once the door was shut behind them, O'Malley hit Zengo upside the head with his webbed hand.

"Have you not learned anything, kid? We have to get that clown on our side. Of course I think he's incompetent. He wouldn't even get through a week of training at the Platypus Police Academy. But we need to have him think that we respect him."

"So what's the plan, then?" asked Zengo.

"The janitor is going to help us."

Zengo looked around. "What?"

"C'mon, let's fill these toilets with as much toilet paper as we can."

Zengo had learned not to question his partner when he had a plan. He entered the first stall and started unraveling the paper off the roll and dumping

it into the toilet bowl. O'Malley did the same in the neighboring stall.

"Now what?" called Zengo from over the stall wall.

"Now we flush and stand back!"

Both Zengo and O'Malley flipped the flush handles. O'Malley had a wide grin on his bill.

The toilet water began to overflow and pool on the floor as the toilet paper clogged the drain.

The guard was eating the last bites of his tuna sandwich when Zengo and O'Malley came bursting back into his office. "I hate to tell you this," said O'Malley, "but the toilets are overflowing in there. There's water everywhere."

The security guard rolled his eyes and got up from his chair. "You've got to be kidding me!" He grabbed his walkie-talkie and spoke into it. "Charlie, come in, Charlie, we've got a situation over here in the security offices. Toilets are overflowing."

The janitor's voice crackled over the radio. "Again? Okay, I'll be right over."

By the time the janitor made it over with his mop and plunger, the water had seeped underneath the bathroom door and was spilling into the hallway. The guard followed him into the bathroom. O'Malley and Zengo quietly rushed back to the main security office.

"Quick! We don't have much time!" O'Malley used his claw as a pick to open the filing cabinet to the right of the guard's desk. A few clicks later the cabinet was open. He rummaged through some files. "Bingo!" he said as he pulled out a batch of folders and hustled to the door. "Just grab as many as you can!" he said.

Zengo scooped up what was left.

"Here, put everything in this crate," instructed O'Malley.

The detectives peered out of the office. They could hear the guard down the hall, still in the bathroom, arguing with the janitor about the best way to handle the mess.

"Hey, it wasn't my fault the toilets were stuffed with TP. Somebody's gotta learn to use just a few squares!"

It was time to get a move on before the guard caught on to their ruse. Zengo opened the door for O'Malley, who was carrying the crate. They slipped outside and almost got away unnoticed.

"Hey! Where you boys goin'? Why'd you clog the toilets?!" shouted the guard. "What are you carrying? I thought I told you boys that was confidential material!"

"Get goin', kid!" shouted O'Malley as he pushed Zengo out into the parking lot. The detectives raced to their squad car, O'Malley clutching the precious crate of files. Zengo unlocked the driver's side door for O'Malley.

Just then a loud engine roared. Zengo turned to see a motorcycle bearing down on them. Before he could even react, the helmeted motorcyclist grabbed the crate out of O'Malley's hands and zoomed toward the parking-lot exit at full throttle.

"Crikes!" shouted O'Malley, hopping in the car. "Get in, rookie, and hold on!" O'Malley turned the car engine on and buckled his seat belt with one swift

motion. By the time Zengo had fastened his own belt, O'Malley already had the car in drive. He floored the gas pedal.

Zengo shouted into the megaphone. "Halt! This is the Platypus Police Squad!" He popped the siren onto the roof, and at a nod from O'Malley turned it on.

"What do you think is in those files?" shouted O'Malley.

"Let's make sure we live to find out!" said Zengo, holding on to the dashboard for dear life as O'Malley picked up speed.

"Here we go, kiddo!" As O'Malley sped toward the exit, the metal security gates began to close. The mystery motorcyclist zipped through.

O'Malley tightened his grip on the steering wheel, then jerked it sharply, sending the car onto its left wheels and just managing to squeeze through the gates before they slammed shut.

The siren screamed as O'Malley threw the car into reverse, spun it around, and threw it back in drive, flooring the gas once more. The car screeched forward and fishtailed into the flow of traffic. Incredibly, they didn't hit anyone or anything.

Zengo could still see the motorcyclist, but he was moving away fast. He grabbed the radio. "This is Detective Rick Zengo calling from car one-fifty-three. We need backup immediately. We are in hot pursuit of a motorcycle heading eastbound on Twelfth Avenue away from the Kalamazoo City Dome. The driver is carrying material sensitive to our investigation. Requesting immediate backup. There is no apparent license plate on the vehicle; I repeat, no license plate."

O'Malley weaved their car in and out of both lanes of traffic. Cars headed in both directions began to move to the side of the road. "C'mon, rook. It's go time!"

Zengo's heart raced. He had seen some action in the

few months he had been on
the force, but he had never
been in a full-on car chase
before. Though they were
going crazy fast, he felt like he
was in a dream, almost as though
they were moving underwater. He had
watched every cop movie ever made, but nothing had ever gotten his adrenaline running like this.
They were tearing through the streets at top speed.
Innocent lives could be lost at the slightest miscalcu-
lation. For once, he was thankful that O'Malley was in
the driver's seat.

The motorcyclist drove off the road and into a busy sidewalk market. The crowd parted to let him through, and then closed up again. They could not follow him with their car. O'Malley screeched to a halt and punched the dashboard in frustration. Zengo popped his seat belt, threw open the door, and began chasing the perpetrator on foot. *We need to get this guy off the road before somebody gets hurt.*

The motorcyclist hit another wall of afternoon shoppers, and Zengo saw his chance. He ran around to flank the motorcyclist, whose only choice was to turn down a dead-end alley. *What an idiot*, Zengo thought, sprinting in after him. The cyclist had turned

his bike around and was facing Zengo, as though he was taunting him to come closer.

Zengo reached for his boomerang just as the perpetrator revved up his engine and zoomed up a wooden plank resting against a Dumpster. The motorcyclist popped a wheelie and launched himself up into the air, clearing the Dumpster and landing on the low roof of a building beside the alley.

As Zengo stood frozen and gaping in astonishment, the motorcyclist pulled out a silver boomerang. It sparkled in the sunlight.

"Kid, duck!" shouted O'Malley as he huffed onto the scene and tackled Zengo. The boomerang hit the ground just where Zengo had stood a second before. From the ground, the detectives watched the cyclist drive across the roof and disappear.

Zengo had had his chance, and he'd blown it. Even worse, he'd been saved by the old-timer. He had never felt more like a rookie detective. He stood up and kicked a trash can, knocking it against the brick wall. "Darn it! I was sure I had him!"

O'Malley thumped his partner on the shoulder.

"Don't beat yourself up, kid. Look around you. No one was hurt. You did what you could do. We put an APB out on this guy. The PPS will catch him."

Zengo shivered at the thought of what just happened. He had always dreamed of action like this, and had always imagined he'd come out looking like a hero. As Zengo watched his short and stubby partner brush off his wrinkled clothes, he realized that O'Malley might be old and out of shape, but he never hesitated when the going got tough.

Zengo pursed his bill and exhaled as he stared at the spot on the roof where the daredevil motorcyclist had taken his shot.

The detectives returned to the Kalamazoo City Dome security offices just as the security guard was being loaded into a squad car, presumably for questioning. The parking lot was filled with cruisers, flashing lights, and blaring sirens. Officers of every ilk had descended upon the scene, prepared for battle. Zengo and O'Malley watched as Sergeant Plazinski took full command of the situation. Just as they were arriving, a tall and lean Dome security officer extended a paw to Plazinski.

"Sergeant Plazinski? Captain Jake Mitchell. I head up security at the Dome and I am horrified by what just happened."

"What are your employees hiding, Captain?" barked Plazinski. "Why were my boys denied access to your records?"

"I'm sorry. I would never instruct my guards to obstruct justice. That guard will be replaced immediately." The feline looked from Plazinski to O'Malley and Zengo, and then back to Plazinski. If this guy wasn't telling the truth, he was sure a convincing actor. *Perhaps he should be shooting a movie here too*, thought Zengo.

Mitchell continued, "My team and I are fully committed to cooperating with the Platypus Police Squad."

"Right you are," snapped Plazinski. "And you're coming to the station to answer a few questions alongside your friend there."

"I, of course, will be more than amenable to assisting you in your investigation," purred the chief of security.

A Lincoln Town Car with tinted windows rolled onto the scene. It came to a stop right before Plazinski. Out stepped Mayor Saunders. Before Plazinski could blow his lid, Saunders held up his wing.

"I cannot apologize enough for the shortcomings of the security team here at the Dome," said the mayor smoothly.

"You mean to tell me you *didn't* instruct the security force to withhold information?" Plazinski spat.

"Of course not. I genuinely thought that Captain Mitchell had everything under control here." The mayor and the captain eyed each other with mistrust.

"Well, clearly they didn't, Mayor," continued Plazinski. "There's obviously something going on here. I'm just glad that I didn't listen to your requests to let this situation sort itself out."

"I owe you my most humble apology, Sergeant. Please know that one weak link does not represent the entire team here at the Dome."

"We'll see about that, Mr. Mayor. I'll be assigning my own officers to the Dome immediately. There will be a member of the PPS on the ground here twenty-four-seven."

Plazinski lumbered off toward his car. He turned back to look at the mayor as he opened the door. "Oh, and by the way, Mr. Mayor—say cheese."

Derek Dougherty was there with his camera, and started snapping photos. "A few words, Mr. Mayor. Is it true that the Dome security force has gotten in the way of a Platypus Police Squad investigation?"

The mayor's assistant stepped forward and held his hand toward Derek's camera. "There will be no questions at this time!"

Zengo felt a tug at his arm. "C'mon, kid. We could use a good hot dog after all this."

"But didn't you just have a—"

"Never you mind, kid. I'm hungry. Let's get outta here."

FRANK'S FRANKS, 2:50 P.M.

O'Malley ordered four dogs with extra chili. Zengo watched, amazed. *Everyone works through stress in his own way*, he thought.

"What do you want, rook?" said O'Malley. "It's my treat."

Zengo looked over the menu. Not much here that anyone would consider healthy.

"I'll take the tofu dog, just ketchup, please."

O'Malley glared at his partner. "You serious? Fine. Whatever." O'Malley turned to the pimpled teenager working the booth. "I'll have a tofu dog for my friend here. Maybe a side of bark and an order of twigs while you're at it."

"Hey, I'm just watching out for my heart, old-timer. Maybe you should do the same."

O'Malley paid for the dogs and took his number slip. "Yeah? A lot of good your salads and tofu did you back in that alley."

Zengo really didn't have an answer for that. He searched for the right words, so as to not sound wimpy in front of his partner. "Guess I was just taken a bit by surprise."

"Rule number one, rookie. Always expect surprises. You don't act fast, you're no good to no one."

The pimpled teenager spoke into a microphone. "Number thirty-two, your order is ready, number thirty—"

"I'm right here, pal." O'Malley threw his number down on the counter and grabbed his tray. The detectives walked across the square and sat at a nearby bench, shaded by the neighboring park's trees. O'Malley scrunched up his nose as he picked up Zengo's tofu dog.

Zengo sighed. "Just give it here."

O'Malley held one of his chili dogs in his webbed

hand and considered it for a moment. "Ya know, rook, it ain't easy doing what we do. I'm sorry I gave you a hard time back there. Anyone can freeze up in the moment."

"You didn't."

"Well, I have a bit more experience with this kind of thing than you do. Enough to know that I can trust myself in situations like that. You should do the same."

"Got it," said Zengo, taking a bite of his tofu dog.

O'Malley lifted his dog. Chili oozed out of the bun and onto his lap. "Aw, crud!" O'Malley reached for napkins and attempted to clean up the mess.

"Hey, Jonathan, isn't that your dad?"

It was O'Malley's middle son, flanked by a gang of giggling teenage boys. O'Malley raised his hand to wave.

"Hey, Johnny! How was school?"

All the boys chimed in unison.

"Johnnnny?"

Jonathan looked horrified

at the sight of his dad furiously trying to clean the inseams of his pants. "Ugh! Dad! You know I go by Jonathan now!"

O'Malley stood up and walked toward his son. "Sorry, Jonathan." He reached out to pull the kid in for a big hug. Now Jonathan really looked horrified.

"Okay, whatever, Dad, chill." Jonathan took a few steps backward.

"Where's your brother?" O'Malley asked. "I thought you were walking him home after school." Jonathan nodded his head back to the hot-dog stand. Declan, Corey O'Malley's youngest, was ordering up a few dogs. *Like father, like son*, thought Zengo as he watched Declan devour the dogs while he approached the group.

"Dad! Jonathan's friends didn't believe me when I told them that you know Chase Mercy!" Declan took the last bite of his hot dog. "Go on, tell 'em!"

"Do you really?" asked one of the boys.

"Well, I did," said O'Malley.

"Cool!" said one of the boys.

"Do you think you could get us his autograph when he comes to town?" asked another.

"He totally can. Right, Dad?" Jonathan asked.

O'Malley puffed up his chest. "Sure, Jonathan. Though I had to admit, back when I knew him, I never would have thought I'd one day be asking Chadwi— Chase Mercy for his autograph."

O'Malley's walkie-talkie went off. It was Plazinski. "O'Malley! Come in, O'Malley!"

O'Malley grabbed the radio. "Sorry, kids, duty calls." He sat down next to Zengo and spoke into his radio. "O'Malley here."

"We shook down the guard. Looks like the mayor and the Dome security captain weren't just feeding us malarkey. This guy is a real piece of work. We're not getting anything out of him, and we can't hold him any longer without charges."

"Hmpph," said O'Malley.

"Clearly that guy was trying to hide something from us," said Zengo.

"We also questioned Jake Mitchell. Not a single member of his team is a rat, physically speaking."

"Sure as hay are a bunch of rats in the figurative sense," grumbled O'Malley. "And what about the motorcyclist? Anyone pick him up?"

"Nowhere to be found," said Plazinski. "But we have every police outfit in the state looking for him."

"They won't have much to go on," complained Zengo.

Plazinski cut Zengo's pity party short. "I'm going to need you boys to make a trip out to Walhalla. Go out and talk to the mayor's Dream Team. After this security debacle, I want to know everything there is to know about the people chosen to work the Dome project. Somebody has it out for Kalamazoo City and I want to know who!"

"Roger that, Sergeant!" O'Malley returned his walkie-talkie to his jacket's inner pocket.

"So, we're after a rat in Walhalla?" asked Zengo as O'Malley scarfed his last two chili dogs.

"Yup. Only problem is—that city is full of 'em."

"It'll be like finding a needle in a haystack."

"More like a needle in a needle stack. C'mon, kid. Let's get a move on."

HIGHWAY 70 WESTBOUND, 3:20 P.M.

The Kalamazoo City skyline shrank in the rearview mirror as detectives Corey O'Malley and Rick Zengo drove to Walhalla. The road between the rival cities was nearly empty. They would get to Walhalla with plenty of time to interview the suspects before the end of the workday.

Zengo stared out the window at the dull suburban landscape, brightened only by flashy billboards bragging about Frank Pandini Jr.'s various businesses. He kept replaying the day's events in his mind, sick to think of how many ways he had blown his chance to

CHASE MERCY IS: SPY MASTERSON!

prove he was more than just a rookie.

Zengo always used to imagine that being a cop would be just like being in a Chace Mercy movie. Ever since he was a kid, he dreamed of the day that *he'd* be the one kicking down doors to take out the bad guys, slapping the cuffs on anyone who dared to pull a boomerang on him. He had played the scene in his mind a million times: no sooner would a perp's boomerang be drawn than Zengo would, with one quick motion, knock the boomerang out of commission and bring the punk's nose to the pavement.

Yet when the big moment came, he froze. He lost his nerve. It was his partner, out of shape and twice Zengo's age, who displayed quick thinking and fearlessly ran toward danger. Zengo knew O'Malley had seen a ton of action in his day. But he had assumed those days were behind him. It was another reminder not to jump to conclusions.

O'Malley pulled the car into the fast lane. He

rolled down his window and flipped on the radio. As always, it was set to the classic-rock station. But then O'Malley switched it to Z94.3, Zengo's favorite hip-hop station, the one O'Malley usually called "noise." Zengo looked sideways to his partner, who didn't take his eyes off the road. The voice of Zengo's favorite DJ, Monte Belmonte, blasted out of the car speakers. Was O'Malley trying to cheer him up?

"Hey, Z94.3 listeners! YOU could be in the next Chase Mercy movie! That's right, Kalamazoo City is becoming Kalamazoolywood when our hometown hero returns to film the next installment of Chase's blockbuster film franchise at the brand-new Kalamazoo City Dome! Caller seven wins the chance to be an extra in the movie! And stay tuned for a brand-new Scam Jam right after I spin this new track from G-Jellyfish. Z94.3, your only source for today's biggest beats!" The car filled with deep percussive bass, followed by auto-tuned rhymes laid over synthesized rhythms.

Zengo was feeling better already. "I didn't realize you were such a big fan of current music there, Corey."

"Hey, I can be hip," O'Malley said.

Zengo smirked. "No, you can't."

O'Malley smiled. "Okay, you're right. But sometimes

"that Monte character cracks me up."

"Man, when I was a platypup, I would have given anything to appear in one of Chase Mercy's movies!"

"Well, we all know you have a mug that was made for the silver screen there, dreamboat," ribbed O'Malley.

"Hey, don't hate the player," chuckled Zengo.

"I can't believe . . . Nobody ever would have pegged Chadwick Mickleheimer for international stardom. If you asked me to pick one person in this whole city who was going to become an action hero, he's the last one I would have chosen."

"Well, it wouldn't be the first time you had someone pegged wrong," Zengo said with a smile.

"Maybe you're right. It's not like I ever really got to know the kid. He always just sat off to the side with an angry look on his face, snapping at anyone who tried to talk to him. To tell you the truth, Squirt was a bit of a jerk."

Their conversation was interrupted by Monte Belmonte, back on the air. "All right, caller number seven, you are the lucky winner. What's your name?"

"Hello? Am I caller number seven?" asked a voice Zengo had just heard in person.

"Yeah, dude! You need to get those ears cleaned! What's your name, kid?"

"Oh, WHOA! Awesome! This is Jonathan O'Malley!"

"WHAAAAT?" screamed O'Malley, clutching the steering wheel so hard he made the car swerve.

"Well, Jonathan, you just earned your way onto the set and into the next Chase Mercy movie. Whaddaya think about that?!"

"Oh man! Oh man! I am so excited! Chase Mercy is the best! He's totally my hero, dude!"

Zengo didn't know Jonathan all that well, but he had never heard him this excited. He was even more excited than the time Zengo let the kid try on his lucky leather jacket.

"Jonathan O'Malley, what's your number one source for today's bumping beats?"

"Z94.3!"

"All right, listeners, you've been warned, it's time for a Scam Jam!"

Zengo turned down the radio. "So, O'Malley, looks like your kid is going to be in the Chase Mercy movie."

"Like heck he is," sneered O'Malley.

"What was all that talk about getting to know people better?" asked Zengo.

"That was before," said O'Malley. "Now that my kid's mixed up in this, he's nothing but a good-for-nothing phony. And besides, they're filming at the Dome, and it ain't safe there."

Zengo smiled. "Right. But remember the whole we're-trying-to-make-the-Dome-safe thing?"

"Honestly, I wouldn't mind if the Dome got dismantled and sold for spare parts," said O'Malley. "At least that way the city would recoup some of the money wasted on that junk pile. And Chase Mercy is nothing but a chump."

O'Malley switched over to the classic-rock station and stepped on the gas, while Zengo dropped the subject and tried to block out the music. It wasn't easy—it reminded him of being in a dentist's chair. How could anyone listen to this stuff? It belonged in a time capsule, not in a twenty-first-century squad car.

"We'll be right back with more groovy hits after a few words from our sponsors."

Another familiar voice came across the radio, in an ad Zengo had heard so often on Z94.3 that he practically knew it by heart. He was surprised to hear it played on Radio Old Fogey.

"Hi, this is Frank Pandini Jr. Don't you deserve the best out of life? My five-star restaurant Black and White serves the best fish in Kalamazoo City, as voted on by Kagat's. Or head to Bamboo and enjoy the best root-beer float in town and a swank nightclub atmosphere. Pandini Enterprises is here to serve. Your life, better!"

Finally the Walhalla skyline was in sight. Walhalla was stuck on itself—filled with snooty people who looked down their noses at the hardworking people of Kalamazoo City. Having once sworn he would never return, Zengo was nonetheless proud to be there in his official capacity. It was time to get some answers from Mayor Saunders's Dream Team.

"Let's prep a little, rook," said O'Malley.

Zengo opened his laptop. "First stop, Audrey Davis, tourism guru. Second stop, Walhalla University. We'll visit a class taught by Dr. Frederick Treeger, one of the world's leading experts on amusement park rides. . . ."

"And the designer of the rides at the Kalamazoo City Dome," said O'Malley.

"Exactly," said Zengo. "According to the registrar's office, he's the most popular professor at W.U."

O'Malley chuckled. "Who wouldn't want to take a class from a guy who's behind the next generation of loop-de-loops?"

"And last, we're going try to track down Maurice Robertson, head of Robertson and Sons Construction."

"That's the crew that built the Disaster Dome," said O'Malley.

"Exactly," said Zengo. "And according to my dad, the Dome is only the latest disaster Robertson is responsible for. Even so, he always seems to land the big fish."

"You sure your dad isn't just a tiny little bit jealous of Robertson's success?" asked O'Malley.

Zengo considered. His dad's construction firm had fallen on hard times in recent years. Maybe he wasn't giving Robertson a fair shake. "It's possible," he said.

"I'll hold off my judgments until we can gather our own information."

"That's the way to go, rookie," said O'Malley. "You're catching on. Good boy."

Zengo clamped his bill shut. He would show O'Malley what he was made of. Then maybe O'Malley would stop calling him rookie once and for all.

STRIVE INC. MAIN OFFICES, 3:40 P.M.

"Ms. Davis, two gentlemen to see you," said the office manager as she opened the doors to Audrey Davis's sprawling corner office. The tourism guru was hunched over a scale model of a miniature golf course. What was she promoting—an amusement park for insects? Zengo looked around the room. There were some other models showcased in Davis's office—a miniature version of the Kalamazoo City Dome, a miniature version of an upscale mall.

"Well, well. Two of Kalamazoo City's finest. A bit of an oxymoron, I know, but a pleasure to meet

you, gentlemen." Audrey
extended her wing for a
shake.

Zengo could see
that O'Malley was
seething from the insult,
but he knew they wouldn't
get anywhere by fighting. He
reached out and shook her wing. "I'm Rick
Zengo and this here's my partner, Corey O'Malley. We
were hoping that we could chat with you for a bit."

"Well, Officers . . ."

"Detectives," O'Malley interrupted.

"Detectives, whatever," said Audrey. "I have a few
minutes, but there is an important meeting coming up.
I'm working on a campaign for a big mini-golf course
and we're locking down the designs today."

"A big mini-golf course? Ha! Now *that's* an oxymoron," said O'Malley.

"What brings you two all the way to Walhalla?"
Audrey asked as she sauntered over to the refrigerator she kept next to her desk. "Could I get either of
you a drink?"

"No, thank you," Zengo said.

"Sure, I'll take a seltzer, please," asked O'Malley. Audrey opened the fridge. There were seltzers, juices, waters—and wheels upon wheels of cheese.

O'Malley probably wasn't even thirsty. He just wanted a chance to see what was inside her refrigerator. Hadn't he told Zengo time and time again that clues are everywhere? Zengo scanned the room to see if there was anything else of interest. But what more did he need to find? A refrigerator full of cheese was highly suspicious all by itself. Or perhaps just strange.

"We wanted to ask you about the Dome," said O'Malley, popping open the can of seltzer.

"Ah, the Kalamazoo City Dome!" Audrey nodded, a smile freezing on her face. "Off to a bumpy start. But mark my words: from the publicity standpoint, it will ultimately be one of my finest accomplishments. What do you need to know? I'll tell you whatever I can, as long as you don't ask me to reveal any trade secrets. I didn't become the nation's number one tourism guru by giving those away for free!"

"We're not really concerned about your PR campaign, but about how you were chosen to run it," said O'Malley. He stood up and paced around Audrey's office, pausing to admire the handiwork of each scale model as he did so. "It's just that folks from Walhalla aren't usually quick to contribute their services to the

benefit of Kalamazoo City. Why would you want to run a campaign to bring more tourism there?"

"A job is a job, gentlemen. It's as simple as that. I didn't get to where I am today by turning down high-profile work."

"You must have had to beat out a lot of competition for the job," said O'Malley as he brought his bill down close for a better look at the scale model of Kalamazoo City Dome. "This really is impressive stuff."

"Thank you. Well, those models were created by the design team over at Robertson and Sons. Nothing but the best for this project."

Second best, thought Zengo, thinking bitterly about his father, whose firm never even got to bid on the Dome project.

"As for landing the job, well . . . we here at Strive don't need to compete for jobs. We haven't bid on a job in years. No, Mayor Saunders came to us himself," said Audrey. "In fact, Mayor Saunders is an old friend. We went to college together. So really, it wasn't a question of if I'd get the job, but when I would start brainstorming slogans to put on billboards."

"You went to school in Kalamazoo City?" asked Zengo.

"I most certainly did not," she laughed with scorn, and gestured to a pennant on the wall. "Eddie and I went to Walhalla University. We even lived in the same dorm freshman year."

Zengo caught O'Malley's eye. "Eddie?" he mouthed.

Audrey's office manager opened the office doors. "Ms. Davis, the Putt-Putt Corporation representatives are here to see you."

"Thanks, Janice," said Audrey, standing. "Please send them right in. We're all done here, right, Detectives? Thanks for your visit. Please do feel free to stop by whenever you are in town."

116

"Did we just get kicked out?" Zengo said to O'Malley as they shuffled into the elevator and pressed *L* for lobby.

"I can't think of another way to interpret what happened."

There was no doubt. They had been dissed. As they rode down in the elevator, Zengo began to spin scenarios.

"Did you see what was in her refrigerator?" he asked.

"You bet I did."

"Are you thinking what I'm thinking?"

"I'm thinking albatrosses don't eat a whole lot of cheese."

WALHALLA UNIVERSITY MAIN CAMPUS, 4:45 P.M.

Zengo and O'Malley sneaked into the back of an audi-
torium that was filled with at least three hundred
students. Some were taking copious notes. Others
were trying to hide their cell phones as they sent text
messages to friends. Still others were fully asleep at
their desks. Based on the droning tone of the professor at the front of the classroom, and the whiteboard
filled with complicated equations, Zengo figured
Intro to Roller Coasters 101 was not the easy A that
O'Malley had assumed it would be.

The detectives took seats in the back row. Zengo

tried to understand what Professor Treeger was talking about. But he might as well have been speaking in a foreign language.

"And so, a roller coaster is able to keep its passengers in their seats thanks to the centrifugal force brought upon by both the speed and the direction in which the car is traveling. Now, I wouldn't suggest you ride without a seat belt. There are portions of a track where you most certainly will fall out and plummet to your doom. But the principles of physics that make the roller coaster so fun are also the same ones that keep the rider safe. Scientifically speaking, it would be more of a challenge to make a roller coaster car stop upside down halfway through a loop than it would be to build one that works properly!"

Professor Treeger laughed nervously and glanced up. Did his gaze settle directly on Zengo and O'Malley? He continued. "Aside from the fascinating physics involved in constructing a loop-de-loop, it makes for a heck of a thrill ride. And in the end, after all of these equations and numbers, that is what designing amusement park rides is all about."

He quickly looked at his watch. "My, look at the time. Please read the next chapter of your textbooks and be prepared for a short quiz in our next meeting. Class dismissed; have a *thrilling* day, people."

Zengo walked with O'Malley to the front of the classroom as the crush of students flowed the other way. *I'd be running out of here, too.* When they reached the professor, he was madly shoving too much paperwork into a too-small briefcase.

"Professor Treeger?" asked O'Malley, flashing his badge.

"Um, yes, that—that is me," said the professor, not meeting O'Malley's gaze.

"We were hoping to ask you a few questions," said Zengo.

"I'm terribly sorry, but I am late, late, late," said the professor as he threw on his coat and grabbed his briefcase.

"That's cool, we can walk with you," said Zengo as he strode alongside the hurried teacher.

O'Malley stepped up along the other side of Professor Treeger as they entered the hallway. "We're mobile!" he said with a grin. "Some fascinating stuff back there, teach."

"Yes, well, thank you," said Professor Treeger as he pushed open the doors to the parking lot. "I'm passionate about what I do."

"And you're good at it, too. I've seen the rides at the new Kalamazoo City Dome, and they're—"

"If you think that I had anything to do with the fiasco on the Dome's opening night"—the professor cut Zengo off—"I can assure you that I did not."

"Who said anything about the opening night?" asked O'Malley.

"I take pride in what I do. I—I—I am horrified by wh-wh-what happened that night."

"We all are," continued O'Malley in a reasonable tone. "And we're trying to get to the bottom of what went wrong. Since you're the guy who designed the attractions, we thought you might have some insight into what happened. We heard what you said up there, about making a roller coaster stop upside down. Do you know that's exactly what happened at the Dome opening night?"

"Um, I can't say I heard that specifically, no. I read

about the fires in the newspaper. Look, I'm late for a meeting with the dean." Professor Treeger unlocked his car and opened the door. "Good evening, Detectives." And with that, Frederick Treeger got behind the wheel, turned on the ignition, and drove off.

"Crazy old kook," said Zengo.

"I'll say. He was pretty jumpy."

"Something tells me that he's not used to dealing with detectives sniffing around his territory."

"I'm not sure he's used to dealing with people much in general."

"You think he's behind the Dome Disaster?"

"Too soon to tell," said O'Malley as they got into their car. "And we can't rush to conclusions just based on the fact that he was acting squirrely. I know we've only just started checking out the professor, but so far, I'm not seeing a clear motive." O'Malley looked at the setting sun in the rearview mirror as they got onto the highway. "One more stop," he said.

Zengo opened his laptop. "Maurice Robertson is building that new MegaMall on the old Walhalla-Kalamazoo City Byway." He shook his head. "Isn't *one* MegaMall enough for this cheesy town?"

O'Malley smirked. "Since when has that ever stopped anyone?"

ROBERTSON AND SONS CONSTRUCTION SITE, OLD WALHALLA-KALAMAZOO CITY BYWAY, 6:00 P.M.

"Look at the size of this construction site!" said Zengo when the signs emblazoned with the Robertson and Sons logo came into view.

O'Malley brought the car to a crawl. "Quite the MegaMall."

"Pretty upscale, based on the stores they'll be putting in," said Zengo, motioning to the logos on the coming-soon sign. "People in Walhalla must have cash to burn."

O'Malley stopped the car and threw it in park.

Both detectives stepped out onto the scene. The sky was growing darker, but floodlights lit the construction site like it was noon on a summer day. Workers crawled over the landscape like ants at a picnic, carrying supplies, running construction vehicles, and building a consumer's dreamscape brick by brick.

"Do you think Maurice is here?" asked O'Malley. "Or in a comfy office somewhere?"

"Oh, he's here all right," said Zengo, gesturing to a large black SUV with tinted windows and a Walhalla University bumper sticker. "I'd know that gas guzzler of his anywhere. It's in all of the publicity shots for Maurice's projects."

They walked over to a trailer compound. "I'll bet our boy is in there somewhere calling the shots," said O'Malley.

"Unless he's already headed home to his mansion," said Zengo.

O'Malley gave Zengo a sideways glance. "Well, we haven't been to his house; we don't know how big it is. Let's not jump to conclusions."

For the second time that day, Zengo clamped his bill shut. At least O'Malley hadn't called him rookie that time.

They found the construction magnate standing at a long table outside the largest of the trailers. Maurice Robertson loomed over a set of blueprints and barked orders to a ragtag group in hard hats. "I want that dry-wall installed in the south end of the mall before the end of the week!"

"That shouldn't be a problem," said O'Malley. "We plan on working overtime, so long as we get time and a half for wages."

Maurice looked up to find two Platypus Police Squad badges in his face. "Mall's not open yet, guys. Come on back in a few weeks."

"A few weeks? Seems like an awfully quick turnaround to get an entire mall up and running," said O'Malley.

"That's what we do at Robertson and Sons Construction. We get it done, on time and on budget."

"You mean you cut corners and use cheap materials?" said Zengo.

Robertson glared at Zengo. "You're Zengo's kid, aren't you?" he said. "The resemblance is unmistakable."

"So what if I am?" said Zengo. "That's not why I'm here." He was going to say more, but he caught O'Malley's warning look.

"I'm sorry, but I have a mall to build. I don't have time to sit and chat." Maurice strode off toward the construction site. His team hustled after him, Zengo and O'Malley hot on their heels.

"You seem like you're kind of in a hurry," said O'Malley, panting as he kept pace. "That's pretty typical for you, isn't it?"

Robertson stopped, turned, and glared at O'Malley. "What are you getting at, copper?" he said.

"Detective," corrected O'Malley. "We're trying to get to the bottom of what went wrong opening night of the Kalamazoo City Dome. And who better to ask than the guy who built it?"

"Most of that falls under the heading of trade secrets," said Robertson. "And I'm not about to give away any of those to Zengo's kid." He guffawed and punched Zengo in the shoulder. "But then again, who am I kidding? What is your dad going to do? Build a six-story pyrotechnics tower into his next kitchen project?" The guys in hard hats chuckled. Zengo remained silent, but didn't break eye contact with the construction mogul.

"You sure get a lot of high-profile jobs," said O'Malley, nodding to the in-progress shopping mecca. "How do you find time to get all of them built, on time and on budget?"

"I land a lot of projects because I'm the best. I'm sure Zengo's old man could tell you that, right, Detective?"

Though Zengo was getting hot under the collar, he kept his cool.

"Well, with all due respect to my partner's dad, yes, your reputation precedes you," said O'Malley. "But what would a proud Walhallian want with a job in Kalamazoo City? When there's clearly so much business in Walhalla?"

"What contractor wouldn't jump at the opportunity to construct a playground like the Dome? Not to mention the spectacular challenge of constructing a retractable roof to make the park accessible year-round? This was a contractor's dream."

"Well, reports are coming in that the roof actually doesn't work," said O'Malley.

"Nonsense!" replied Maurice defensively.

"It's true," O'Malley continued. "Word on the scene was that the cause of the smoke and fire damage was the roof's failure to properly retract."

"Listen," said Maurice, his face turning red, "I build these sites based on what I'm given in the blueprints. Maybe you should be talking to that loony bin of an engineer who designed the park! My craftsmanship is unparalleled!"

"Hey, man, don't shoot the messenger," said O'Malley coolly. "I thought you were a part of a Dream Team."

"Ha! Dream Team? Sure, we're all from Walhalla, but that doesn't mean all of us know what we're doing." He checked his watch. "Listen, I don't have time for this. If you want to set up a meeting, call my secretary. I'm on a job right now, and time is money. Besides," said Maurice, tapping his hard hat, "this is a hard-hat-only area. Good evening, Detectives."

The largest member of Maurice's crew stepped forward. "Shall I escort them off the property?"

Zengo waved him off. "Don't worry about us. We'll be just fine."

Zengo and O'Malley turned and made their way to the car.

"Sure doesn't like criticism, does he?" said Zengo.

"Nope," said O'Malley. "And when push came to shove, he sure didn't hesitate to throw one of his colleagues under the bus. Come on, it's been a long day. Let's get some shut-eye and put all these pieces together in the morning."

PLATYPUS POLICE SQUAD HEADQUARTERS, 8:30 A.M.

O'Malley had his feet up on his desk as he sipped his fourth coffee the next morning. Zengo sat across from his partner at his own desk, clicking through websites as they talked. Diaz and Lucinni flanked the detectives on either side. For once, they weren't hurling insults at one another, but laying out possible motives of the suspects that they had.

"The problem," Lucinni said, "is that we don't have any way of tracking down the guy from the photo. Dome security tells us he isn't one of the rats that works for them. The uniform must have been counterfeit."

"Speaking of rats, why would Audrey fill her office fridge with cheese?" pondered O'Malley.

"She could just really like cheese," said Diaz.

"But in her office? It must have been for someone visiting her."

"Maybe some of her clients are mice?" suggested Lucinni.

"None that I can find," said Zengo. He had already combed through Strive's website and looked at their client list. "Still, it's far from conclusive. She has too much to lose if the Dome fails. Why would she take the risk of hiring this guy to sabotage it?"

"She knew the mayor in college. Maybe they had a falling-out?" suggested O'Malley.

"Speaking of Walhalla U, what about the college professor?" asked Lucinni. "He sounds like he was acting rather sketchy."

"But amusement-park rides are his whole life," said Zengo. "How often does he get the chance to build a project of this scale? It's his reputation on the line if the thing goes south. And I'm not seeing any sort of motive here."

134

"Except . . ." said O'Malley, taking the last sip of his coffee. "Do you remember when he talked about the challenge of making a roller coaster stop upside down? Maybe he decided to turn the park into his own little physics experiment."

"You think?" Zengo asked.

"Not sure. It's a little thin, I'll admit. Now, I do think that Maurice Robertson has a thorn or two in his side about our hometown, more so than any of the other Dome players."

"Yeah, he sure had a short fuse," said Zengo. "But would he sabotage the Dome's opening? It seems like he has as much to lose as anyone."

"I don't know about sabotage," said O'Malley. "But we know he's been cutting corners with his work for years. Maybe it finally caught up to him when the Dome broke down, and now he's trying to push the blame onto anyone but himself."

Zengo's phone buzzed. It was a *Kalamazoo City Krier* news alert. "Hey, guys, check this out," he said. "Frank Pandini Jr. has just been announced as a surprise guest on *Kalamazoo City Today*."

"Huh," said O'Malley as they got up from their chairs to scurry to the break room. "Must be some kind of big announcement."

Diaz turned on the set, which filled with the image of the great Frank Pandini Jr. sitting on the famous *Kalamazoo City Today* couch, hot seat for the rich and famous. He sat opposite the host, Jaiden Meltzer.

"Go on," said the host.

"The mayor negligently pushed this Dome project forward," said Pandini. "It was for his own personal gain, not for the good of the city."

"That's a mighty powerful allegation," said Jaiden Meltzer. "I assume you have the facts to back it up?"

"Absolutely," said Pandini. "Everyone knows that as Mayor Saunders headed into his last term, his poll numbers were dangerously low. He had no intention of heading out with his tail feathers between his legs. He saw the Dome as the key to securing his legacy. He'll have his legacy, all right—at the expense of the taxpayer: their lives, possibly; their money, definitely. Even if everything went perfectly, it will take more than TEN YEARS for the Dome to recoup the taxpayers' investment. Now comes this fiasco of an opening. The Dome is doomed—and it will probably take the whole city down with it."

"What should the mayor have done differently?" pressed Jaiden Meltzer.

"For starters, he should have hired a competent team," said Pandini. "Not to mention a local one. Do you know that not a single person involved in the planning and construction of the Dome is from Kalamazoo City? We are sending our hard-earned tax dollars over to Walhalla. And why on earth did the mayor decide to build the Dome on top of the dump? The mayor must think we want our kids playing in a garbage pit. What do you make of that?"

The host looked disgusted and shook his head. Zengo and O'Malley shared a look. Jaiden Meltzer was a popular figure in the city. If Pandini got Meltzer on his side, the mayor was in trouble. As much as Pandini made Zengo's blood burn, he had to admit the guy could work a room—or in this case, a camera.

"Of course not!" continued Pandini. "You don't want that! None of us do!"

"Well, what can we do about it?" asked Jaiden Meltzer.

"Facing this tremendous failure of leadership, I've decided to take matters into my own hands," said Pandini. "I've hired my *own* team of scientists—at my *own* expense, naturally—to test the land down at the Dome. Preliminary findings are very discouraging. All that rotting garbage buried underground is oozing toxic chemicals into the water supply, and the waste from the construction is polluting the air. Mayor Saunders could have used green initiatives, like solar power and other forms of renewable energy, but did he? No. The Dome is a burden on our ecosystem, which was fragile enough before this whole thing started."

"Why have you decided to invest so much of your own money in this, Mr. Pandini?"

Pandini's face grew earnest as only Pandini's could. "Because, Jaiden—I care for this city with every hair on my body. I'm heartbroken by what is going on. I want this city to succeed. I even brokered the deal to bring the next Chase Mercy movie here, no thanks to Mayor Saunders. It's his lack of proper leadership that has brought this shame on our city. And it's time for him to face the music."

"What are you suggesting, Mr. Pandini?" Jaiden Meltzer asked, leaning forward even farther in his chair. Zengo looked down and found that he was doing the same.

Pandini sat back in his chair, and said calmly, "I think it's high time Mayor Saunders stepped down."

THE CORNER OF SOUTH STREET AND KALAMAZOO
BOULEVARD, 10:00 A.M.

By the time O'Malley and Zengo hit the streets that
morning, Chase Mercy mania was at a fever pitch.
Shortly after Pandini finished his television appear-
ance, he announced that he would personally ensure
that no matter what happened with the Dome, the
filming would stay right there in Kalamazoo City.
Everywhere the detectives turned, Chase Mercy's
face was in their faces. Kiosks crammed with maga-
zines, T-shirts, and an array of Chase bling were doing
brisk business on every street corner.

Zengo rummaged through the merchandise arrayed in a cart set up at the corner of South and Kalamazoo. "Hey, O'Malley, how about a Chase Mercy key chain?" he said, nudging his partner. "Or a Chase Mercy pillowcase?"

O'Malley flashed his badge to the street vendor. "You have a license, pal?"

The vendor snatched the pillowcase away from Zengo and hurried off with his loot.

"Heh. Lousy parasites," said O'Malley. "I'm sure Squirt has got plenty of cash already, but it's not right for folks to be making a quick buck off of his mug."

"What? You don't think these guys are giving Mercy a royalty from this 'official' Chase Mercy merchandise?" Zengo smirked.

"No way," said O'Malley as they continued to meander down South Street. They were just blocks from the Dome, staking out the area. Diaz and Lucinni were detailed to shake down the Dome's security staff for any information on the saboteur who was photographed wearing one of their security uniforms.

But it was slow going on South Street. The sidewalk and even the street were clogged by the hordes of Chase Mercy fans who were camped out near the Dome, hoping to catch a glimpse of the superstar.

They stepped around a couple of female fans who had set up lawn chairs and were playing cards to pass the time. Each card, of course, had Chase Mercy's face printed on the back. "Don't you kids have something better to do?" grumbled O'Malley.

Zengo's phone buzzed—it was another news alert. Mayor Saunders was about to hold a press conference at the Dome. "O'Malley, we need to get to the Dome now," he said, showing the text to O'Malley before stuffing the phone back into his pocket.

"There's no way we'll get there in time with all these people clogging the roads." O'Malley pointed to an old appliance store across the street. "Let's head to Barney's and watch it on TV. Glad to see old Barney is still here."

"But not for long, apparently," said Zengo, pointing to the GOING OUT OF BUSINESS sign that hung on the door.

"Aw, crud! Barney's been in business in this neighborhood for years!" said O'Malley.

"Well, it was only a matter of time," said Zengo, pointing to the construction site located directly across from the old-fashioned shop. The logo for TV World—a big-box electronics store—was displayed on the chain-link fence that cornered off the site.

The bell over the creaky door jangled as Zengo and O'Malley walked into Barney's shop. Televisions lined the wall. All were tuned to an animated movie to show off the high-definition screens.

Barney was all smiles as the partners entered.

"O'Malley, yah old lug! What brings you in?"

"Hey, Barney, you mind if we switch the channel

to the news conference the mayor is about to give?" asked O'Malley.

"Fine by me," said Barney, his grin giving way to a scowl, "just don't be offended if I spit at the screen."

"Yeah, the mayor sure is taking a beating in the polls," said Zengo.

"Well, I'm going outta business thanks to his 'forward thinking,'" sneered Barney. "I thought that all the traffic that the Dome would bring to this area would be good for business. And it would be—if the mayor hadn't green-lit the big-box stores coming into this neighborhood at the same time."

"That stinks!" lamented O'Malley.

"Yeah, well—say good-bye to all of the little storefronts around here. Mayor's legislation is gonna be pushin' us all outta business."

Just then, the television screens lit up with images of Mayor Saunders stepping behind the podium. "Greetings, my fellow Kalamazooians. I've come before you to respond to the unfounded, slanderous attacks launched at me by an individual who I thought was a good friend of mine, and of our entire city. I am as shocked as I am hurt by the words that Mr. Pandini Jr. had for me earlier today. The bottom line is—he's wrong. The Dome is on track to bring millions of dollars into Kalamazoo City. Our tourism industry is on the rise, and our city is now a family destination for the whole country, thanks to the Dome. Moreover, the air and water here by the Dome are clean and safe. I don't know where Mr. Pandini is finding these scientists of his, but I sure hope that it isn't from the same place where he's hiring his restaurant employees."

Burn, thought Zengo, remembering his first case,

when the Platypus Police Squad discovered one of Pandini's barbacks at Bamboo was selling illegal fish.

"Now, there has been much talk about Pandini Enterprises and what they have done to bring Chase Mercy's next film to KC. And there is no doubt that Pandini did help to put us in touch with certain people in Hollywood. But it was me, your mayor, who convinced Chase to film his next movie in his hometown. Chase is a citizen that we can all be proud of, just as the Dome is a part of our city we can all be proud of.

"But don't just take my word for it. Please welcome back to Kalamazoo City Mr. Chase Mercy."

Nobody expected this. Chase wasn't expected in town for another week. But here he was, taking the stage and flashing his million-dollar smile, waving to the press covering the event while the huge crowd went crazy. He was inundated by flashes that fired like heavy artillery. He was clearly a pro at this game, what with the countless red-carpet events he had attended over the years.

"Squirt, man," O'Malley said to himself. "I can't believe it." Looking at his old schoolmate must have made O'Malley feel a little insecure about the shape that he was in, thought Zengo. *Here are two guys the same age—one is chubby and balding; the other is lean and handsome.*

"Hello, Kalamazoo City!" said Chase. The reporters on scene erupted in applause. "I am so happy to be back in my hometown. I want to thank you all for being here, and for this fabulous welcome. And I especially want to thank Mayor Saunders for making all of this happen. You know, a lot of important decisions go into moviemaking. And when we were deciding where to film my next Spy Masterson movie—well, Mayor Saunders just made us an offer that we could not refuse. I know that filming in town will require a lot of patience from everyone. Some streets will get closed down from time to time, restaurants will be filled up with our crew, and at times we'll need to close the awesome Dome that Mayor Saunders built. But in the end—it'll all be worth it. Because we will be making Kalamazoo City, the city we all love, a part of film history." More applause erupted.

"Good grief," said O'Malley.

"What? This is exciting," said Zengo.

"I just can't believe little Squirt Mickleheimer is here pretending he loves Kalamazoo City so much.

The way I remember it, he couldn't wait to get out of here the minute he graduated. As if anyone noticed."

Zengo couldn't help but feel a kinship with Chase Mercy, if only because his partner called both of them by offensively belittling nicknames. "Do I detect a bit of jealousy in there, tough guy?"

O'Malley snorted. "No way. I don't need to leave town and come back pretending I'm some kind of hero to be comfortable with who I am." Zengo couldn't help but notice, however, that his partner's gaze had dropped to his feet. "It doesn't matter. Chase Mercy isn't our problem. The Dome is. We need to figure out what's going on here, because it looks like the Dome is going to start drawing crowds again. The mayor knows exactly what he's doing here. He's playing the public like checkers."

"So is Pandini," said Zengo.

"You're right. And I'm afraid of what's going to happen when one of them wins."

KALAMAZOO CITY HALL, 1:00 P.M.

Mayor Saunders's staff had hastily organized a ceremony on the steps of City Hall to bestow the Key to the City on Chase Mercy. Representatives from all of the city's high-school marching bands had been rushed in and were onstage playing the beloved tune "Invincible"— the theme song from the Spy Masterson movies and the new unofficial anthem of Kalamazoo City.

Zengo and O'Malley were perched on the rooftop of an adjacent office building, scanning the crowd with their binoculars. They were opposite Diaz and Lucinni, doing the same thing on a building across the street. Downtown was absolutely mobbed. Kalamazoo City was bursting with fanfare.

"Quite a scene," said Zengo.

"Yeah, the kind of hullabaloo usually reserved for a Sharks World Series championship," said O'Malley.

Zengo put his binoculars down and glared sideways at his partner. "You're lucky, old man. The last time the Sharks went all the way, I hadn't even been born yet."

Zengo had hoped to get a little rise out of O'Malley with that dig. But his partner was unperturbed. "Maybe someday, rookie," said O'Malley as he scanned the crowd.

"Check out who has the best seats in the house," said Zengo, motioning toward the main stage at the top of the stairs at City Hall. Frederick Treeger, Audrey Davis, and Maurice Robertson all perched on choice seats.

"Ah, our old pals," sneered O'Malley.

"Man, folks will stop at nothing to get a little taste of celebrity," said Zengo. "I bet these clowns from Walhalla took the Dome job just to get in on some Chase Mercy action."

"They may all hate on each other behind closed doors, but they sure are happy to smile for the camera," said O'Malley as he watched Derek Dougherty snap photos. Zengo watched in admiration as the amphibian slithered at odd angles to capture more award-winning photographs.

"I wonder how many kids here skipped school," griped O'Malley as he focused his binoculars on a gang of kids.

"The mayor was nuts to hold this during school hours. It's just asking for trouble." Zengo scanned the crowd, but stopped when he saw a familiar face. He didn't want to tell his partner who he saw, but he had no choice. "Uh, hey . . . O'Malley, I hate to tell you this,

but Jonathan is here to see his 'hero.'"

O'Malley's binoculars swerved over to where Zengo was pointing. Jonathan was wearing a ball cap and carried the same backpack he brought to school every morning. The senior O'Malley's blood reached a boiling point. "I'll put him on lockdown for the rest of the school year! He had a test this afternoon! I helped him study!"

"How did he even get out of class?" asked Zengo. "McKeever runs a tight ship over at Kal East."

"Well, we're about to find out. Let's go!" O'Malley

grabbed his walkie-talkie. "Diaz, Lucinni, come in. Do you read me?"

In a moment, Diaz's voice came over the radio. "Ten-four, O'Malley."

"Zengo and I are hitting the street. You have us covered?"

"Roger that," said Diaz. Zengo looked across the street, and Lucinni waved his stubby, webbed hand in the affirmative. Zengo wasn't sure that this was the best way for them to maintain surveillance on the area, but he knew for a fact that there would be no talking O'Malley out of confronting his son.

The two detectives spilled into the city streets among the Chase Mercy fanboys and fangirls, many of whom had dressed up as characters from his movies. O'Malley looked back at Zengo, and pointed to a Kal East baseball hat bobbing ahead in the crowd. He pushed ahead through the sea of people. Zengo was close behind, attempting to keep a low profile. They were, after all, on duty and undercover.

O'Malley finally caught up with the kid. He grabbed him by the shoulder and spun him around. "You are in some serious hot water, son!"

"Dude! What gives?" snapped the kid he'd grabbed.

It was definitely not Jonathan.

"Uh, I, uh . . ." Zengo had never seen O'Malley at such a loss for words. "Sorry 'bout that!" He awkwardly patted the kid on the shoulder.

In the few minutes that it took Zengo and O'Malley to get down from the roof of the building, the crowd had swelled considerably. There was no way they would find Jonathan in this mess. As they got ready to give up, the band stopped.

"Citizens of Kalmazoo City!" boomed Mayor Saunders's voice over the loudspeakers. They looked up to see he was at the podium now, holding up a cartoon-ishly large key. "I am so honored to have you all here today as we bestow the key to our beloved city to our native son—HOLLYWOOD LEGEND CHASE MERCY!"

The crowd roared, but Zengo was confused. There was no way that there was a single keyhole in the entire city where that key could possibly fit.

Chase Mercy walked onto the stage and waved to

the crowd, and the roar grew louder. Man, this guy was good, thought Zengo.

"Keep your eyes on the crowd," whispered O'Malley. "While they're staring at the action hero, we might catch some action of our own. If the saboteur at the Dome was out to squash Chase Mercy's filming, he or she might try something here as well."

Zengo nodded. They both scanned the audience as well as the platform of dignitaries. Then, at the shadowy edge of the pomp and circumstance, Zengo noticed a suspicious-looking character. He poked his partner in the chest. "Lookit!"

O'Malley saw him, too. A chunk was missing from his ear, just like the one in the photo Derek had snapped that night at the Dome. "It's him! It has to be," whispered O'Malley.

"Looks like he's scanning the crowd himself," said Zengo. The guy was looking nervously back and forth. "Let's nab him before it's too late!"

Zengo started to rush forward, but O'Malley grabbed his arm. "No, we've got to sneak up on him. Look at the size of this crowd. If he bolts, we'll lose him!"

Zengo agreed. The suspect was on the far side of the stage. The detectives slowly made their way through the crowd, careful to not get caught. "He's standing pretty close to Chase Mercy's security team. It looks like they don't even notice him," whispered Zengo.

"Maybe they graduated from the same two-bit

security school as the team over at the Dome. Knuckle-heads, I tell ya."

Just then Zengo realized the guy had caught sight of them. For a split second, the two of them made eye contact. Then he made a run for it, slipping to the back of the platform and disappearing.

Zengo had hoped he and his partner would nab this suspect quietly. Wishful thinking. If they wanted to catch him now, Zengo only had one choice. He rushed onto the platform, brushing past the Dream Team. Skittish Frederick leaped out of his seat, knocking into a Chase Murphy statue, which knocked the giant key out of the real Chase Mercy's hand and then sent the podium crashing forward. A piece of the stage collapsed, and Chase Mercy, Mayor Saunders, and the Dream Team all tumbled down after it. The crowd booed as O'Malley leaped over the gap and lumbered past. Zengo caught a momentary glimpse of the crowd. Jonathan O'Malley stood right below the front of the stage. He looked like he was going to vomit—either from embarrassment or fear, Zengo couldn't tell.

Chase Mercy's bodyguard, stationed on the side of the stage, tried to block Zengo. Zengo hip-checked him, landed in a tumble-roll, and sprinted after the saboteur. "Hey, you, stop! Platypus Police Squad!"

O'Malley brandished his badge, but the husky bodyguard, who was twice O'Malley's size, refused to budge. In one move, O'Malley spun around and slapped his tail against the bodyguard's face, knocking him to the ground. O'Malley charged after his partner.

Zengo ran, holding up his badge and yelling for people to get out of his way. But it was hopeless. The crowd was too dense, for one thing. And since he had just wrecked the Chase Mercy party, he hadn't won himself any friends. Nobody was in any hurry to get out of his way. He pushed through the crowd, but there was no hope. The culprit had scurried in between legs and tails and was nowhere in sight.

The rat had flown the coop.

PLATYPUS POLICE SQUAD HEADQUARTERS, 2:45 P.M.

Sergeant Plazinski paced back and forth, back and forth, the length of his window bank. Zengo and O'Malley kept their bills shut and their tails tucked. The fiasco at City Hall was the talk of the town. Zengo had to shut off his cell phone because it kept buzzing with news updates, mainly consisting of images of him and his partner dashing across the stage. Not only were Derek Dougherty's photos displayed prominently on the *Kalamazoo City Krier*'s website, and from there all over the internet, but everybody who snapped blurry photos with their phones had already uploaded those pictures everywhere.

"This is troubling," Plazinski began.

Zengo was sure they were about to be tossed from the case. He glumly considered what his next assignment would be. Which job would be more unpleasant, being a meter maid or cleaning up after police horses?

"Very troubling," Plazinski continued. He stopped, silhouetted by the Kalamazoo City skyline, then spun around to face the detectives. "I think that this fiasco hits closer to Saunders than I feared."

He wasn't mad? Zengo breathed a sigh of relief. He really thought they were going to get their heads handed to them.

"You're certain it was the same guy from the photo?" Plazinski asked.

"He was missing the same chunk from the same ear," said Zengo.

Zengo watched Plazinski gaze out the window, as if he were looking for answers among the skyscrapers.

"It's the best lead that we have," he finally said. "Heck, at this point, it's the only lead we have. But some questions remain. Who was he working for? If it's one of the Dream Teamers, why would someone on the mayor's staff want to sabotage the Dome? If it isn't, who else has it out for the Dome?"

Zengo wished there were room for him to pace too. Everything about this case was pace-worthy.

Abruptly Plazinski changed the subject. "Mayor Saunders is holding a black-tie fund-raiser event tonight at the Dome along with Chase Mercy."

"Sounds fancy," said O'Malley.

"It is. And I want both of you there," said Plazinski.

"You got us on the guest list?" said Zengo, trying to conceal his excitement at the thought of rubbing elbows with Chase Mercy.

"Sort of. Here's your invitation," said Plazinski, handing him a search warrant.

"Gotcha," said Zengo.

"If there's going to be another attempt to embarrass the mayor or mess with the Dome, I'd wager it'll be tonight. I want answers, and I want them immediately. If this investigation goes on any longer, it will unravel. We need to be sure that the Dome is safe. Not only for the citizens of Kalamazoo City, though of course they are our first priority. But also, if Chase Mercy gets hurt on a booby-trapped set, it will be disastrous for our city, our people, and our department."

"Say no more, Sarge," said Zengo, standing up. He and O'Malley pushed aside the orange plastic chairs and started for the door.

"And boys," said Plazinski. "This is a fancy affair. You do have the appropriate evening wear, I hope?"

"You kidding me? I'll look sharper than a steak knife," said Zengo. He looked to his partner.

"Uh . . . of course I do," said O'Malley. Zengo gave him a questioning look. "What?" O'Malley continued. "You don't think I take my wife out for date nights?"

THE KALAMAZOO CITY DOME, 7:30 P.M.

"Okay, so maybe it's been a few years since I've taken Karen out," said O'Malley, attempting to button his jacket.

"A few years or a few decades?" asked Zengo. O'Malley gave up on buttoning his jacket, and tucked his dress shirt into his pants. It looked like a struggle. Zengo stepped out of the car with ease and swagger. His pants were crisp, with a perfect crease on each leg. The cuffs of his stark-white dress shirt stuck out of his tuxedo-jacket sleeves a perfect half inch. Zengo didn't even need to straighten his bow tie. It was tied this detective.

"I guess bright orange was the style back then?" said Zengo, fingering the fabric of O'Malley's tight-fitting jacket while watching his partner try and fail to tie his bow tie.

"Listen, kid, life isn't all nightlife and fancy pants, okay?" sputtered O'Malley.

Zengo thought he could hear O'Malley's blood pressure rise as he once again undid the bow tie to try again.

"Here, let me do it," said Zengo. He bent down and took hold of O'Malley's tie, expertly knotting it around his neck. "Now who's the rookie?" Zengo asked. O'Malley didn't reply.

"Besides, the invite said black-tie."

"Well, what color is this tie, then?" asked O'Malley.

"It's navy blue. But that's not the point. Black-tie event means that you wear a tuxedo."

"Hmpph," said O'Malley as they crossed the parking lot and made for the front gate. "Details."

"Ah, Detectives Rick Zengo and Corey O'Malley! I am surprised to see that you made the guest list." Maurice Robertson approached the instant the two web-footed cops entered the party. The Dome's central square had a tent set up and was lit with moon lanterns. A jazz quartet played in the corner as waitstaff dressed in white tuxedo shirts brought hors d'oeuvres around to all the guests. A waitress carrying a tray of miniature crab cakes stopped before O'Malley and Zengo. Zengo gingerly took one, smiling as he accepted the cocktail napkin the waitress gave him.

"Don't mind if I do!" said O'Malley as he grabbed two fistfuls of crab cakes. Zengo shot him a look sideways. "What? These are tiny! And I missed dinner," said O'Malley with a mouthful of food.

"Yes, we did indeed make the guest list," said Zengo, returning to Maurice Robertson. "Did you enjoy the key ceremony?"

"Not as much as you two clowns did," chuckled the construction tycoon.

Zengo caught sight of Audrey Davis from across the crowded room. She was talking to the mayor and she did not look very pleased to see the two detectives. She came marching straight toward them.

"Good evening, Detectives. Many apologies, but I don't believe that I saw your names on the guest list."

"Oh no?" said O'Malley.

"No. I wrote up the guest list. And I certainly did not include either of you."

"Then why," said Zengo, reaching for his inner jacket pocket, "do we have this?"

Audrey took the search warrant in her wings and inspected it. She handed it back to Zengo, who returned it to his jacket pocket. Audrey looked angrily around the room. "All right. But you had better not bother anyone unless you check with me first."

"Oh, right. We are all still in service of the mighty Audrey Davis," sneered Maurice. "Whatever Audrey says goes." Audrey grabbed Maurice by the arm and escorted him around to the other side of a pillar. Zengo and O'Malley had no choice but to take a step in their direction to eavesdrop.

"Listen, you hack, if it weren't for me, none of us would be here," said Audrey. "This whole project got off the ground because I lifted it onto my back."

"If it weren't for me, we'd all be standing in a junk-yard right now, knee-deep in raw sewage," Maurice shot back.

"*Pffft!* Any contractor worth anything could have leveled this land with a bulldozer. It takes true skill to then convince the public that this was a place they wanted to be. Don't forget, Maurice, I can sell a plate of garbage as a signature dish at a five-star restau-rant. And let's face it—that's what I did with the Dome you built."

"You wouldn't know quality craftsmanship if it bit you in the tail!" said Maurice, his voice getting louder. Zengo watched as Frederick Treeger caught wind of the sparring from across the party and stepped around the pillar.

"I couldn't help but overhear." Treeger's tone was even meaner than the other two. "Can't you both see how incompetent you are? You've both taken my flawless park design and ruined it. The only reason either of you were hired is because of your relationship with the mayor."

"Yes, well some of us are closer to the mayor than others," said Maurice, glaring at Audrey.

"I'm a professional," said Audrey. "I was hired because I deliver to my clients a top-notch public-relations campaign. And what PR maven wouldn't want the challenge of getting people to visit Kalamazoo City? Blech!"

"I'll toast to that," said Maurice, looking around the room. "The dump that I leveled actually looked nice compared to this trashy city."

O'Malley tightened his webbed hands into fists. Zengo patted him on the back. Nobody talked about their city like that and got away with it.

The Kalamazoo City trash-talking was cut off at that moment as Mayor Saunders tapped his spoon against a glass to grab everyone's attention.

"Thank you, thank you! Thank you all for attending this evening's festivities! I just wanted to share a few words. Tomorrow, cameras will begin to roll!" The crowd applauded with measured excitement. The mayor continued, "This means so much for our fair city, on so many levels. Kalamazoo City is entering a renaissance. I am so proud to have shepherded all of this excitement along. The history books will remember this moment in our city's history as a true turning point. So cheers, to the city we all love—to Kalamazoo City!"

"Sure. The history books will certainly remember, but not for the reasons our jolly ol' mayor is hoping for," whispered Zengo.

"History has a way of rewriting itself," grumbled O'Malley.

"Still bitter after all these years, aren't you, Corey?" said a voice from behind them. O'Malley froze. Zengo knew that voice.

It was Chase Mercy.

THE KALAMAZOO CITY DOME, 8:05 P.M.

"How are you, old friend?" Chase held out a paw for a shake. O'Malley obliged.

"Nice to see you, Chadwick," said O'Malley, avoiding eye contact.

Chase narrowed his eyes. "Not quite the person you remember, am I?"

"Not quite. But it's nice to see that you're finally giving something back to your hometown."

"Really? And what do I owe Kalamazoo City?"

"If you had quit your sulking for five minutes, you would have seen that this town was a great place to grow up."

"Don't be so quick to judge, Corey. I didn't have it easy here when I was a kid."

"Drew and I had always asked you to come hang out with us, and you always refused. What could you have possibly had to complain about?"

"Are you looking for a list? You didn't know me at all. You don't know what it was like to grow up in the shadow of Drew Mickleheimer and his best pal, Corey O'Malley. You don't know what it was like to be called Squirt all the time."

The conversation was cut short by the mayor, who was on the mic inviting Chase up to say a few words. He let out an audible sigh. "It never ends," he muttered under his breath as he reluctantly stepped into the spotlight. But once he was in that spotlight, the ear-to-ear smile broke out.

The guy who had just stood before Zengo was nothing like the character he played in the Spy Masterson movies. He was also nothing like the actor who always sounded so confident in interviews.

"What's up with this guy?" asked Zengo. "He's on top of the world, and yet he can't say five words to you without bringing up stuff from twenty years ago?"

"I don't know," said O'Malley. "But I'm tired of all

this malarkey. C'mon, let's step outside and find some food."

Leave it to O'Malley to always know where to get the best grub. He led Zengo to the area outside of the tent where the trays of food had been coming from. The detectives stationed themselves outside of the kitchen door and intercepted the trays of fresh food right out of the kitchen. In no time, O'Malley had a fistful of sushi in one hand, a fistful of mini hot dogs in another.

"These mini hot dogs are cute," he said, "but how could anyone eat just one?"

The detectives stood in the neon glow of the rides, which were all lit up for the night. The park was closed to the public, but a few dozen construction workers and security guards dotted the grounds, testing the rides and getting the park ready for the next day, while location scouts and cinematographers scoured the grounds for the best camera angles. Zengo gazed nervously at the Ferris wheel towering above them.

O'Malley chomped away and Zengo walked over to peer through a seam in the tent. The partygoers were just clinking glasses to the end of Chase Mercy's toast. He jumped down off the stage and made a quick exit as the jazz quartet picked up their instruments and kicked into gear. O'Malley tapped his feet.

"I thought you were all about classic rock," said Zengo, sitting on a discarded milk crate.

"Jazz is a lot like detective work, kid. It's all about improvisation, and it takes a tight crew to pull it off."

"Yeah, but we don't exactly have time for a jam session right now," said Zengo. "The sergeant is going to hang us by the tails if we don't get to the bottom of this case."

"Well, perhaps the bottom of the case will come to us," said O'Malley with a hint of a wink.

"Huh?" Zengo was hushed by O'Malley before he could get another sound out.

Across the square from where the detectives dined, a suspiciously familiar-looking tail peeked out from around a stack of Chase Mercy head-shots.

The detectives crept up around the other side of the tent, careful to remain hidden behind the potted cypress trees that Audrey's company had set up throughout the party.

Soon they were close enough to spot the body that went with that tail. It was a guy in a KC Dome security uniform—a guy who was missing a chunk out of his ear, who had the same steely gaze that had bored holes in Zengo earlier in the day. It was their guy, all right.

It's true, thought Zengo. *Criminals always return to the scene of the crime.* The counterfeit guard even held a wrench that was nearly as big as he was. He was leaning over to speak to someone the detectives couldn't see. Was he planning more sabotage? And who was he talking to? The detectives wouldn't be able to get a glimpse of the other person without giving themselves away. But they were just close enough to be able to listen in on the conversation.

"Just do the job I hired you for," said the voice from the shadows. Whoever it was handed the saboteur a large roll of bills. "Burn this place down!"

THE KALAMAZOO CITY DOME, 8:32 P.M.

"Now!" whispered O'Malley. The detectives leaped from their hiding place, badges in hand, and yelled, "Freeze! Platypus Police Squad!"

The figure holding the money jumped in the air, hundred-dollar bills flying everywhere. Through the rain of cash, Chase Mercy spun around to face the detectives. He had been caught completely off-guard. He didn't try to explain what he was doing; he simply bolted. The saboteur sped off in the opposite direction.

"You go after Mercy; I'll get the little guy!" said

O'Malley. Zengo nodded and took off after the action star.

Zengo could barely run fast enough to keep the suspect in sight. If the guy wasn't an athlete back in the day, he certainly was one now.

Zengo drew his boomerang and shouted, "Stop, or I'll throw!" But Chase Mercy didn't even slow down, much less turn around to look at him. He ran through the ropes and out into the park.

Zengo thought of the last time he had used his boomerang in public. He had caught his perp, but he really could have hurt someone. Chase Mercy was pretty far away, and there were maintenance workers and guards everywhere. Could Zengo take him down at that distance? He couldn't risk it.

Zengo picked up his pace. Even if the superstar was in shape, he was twice as old as Zengo. Eventually he would run out of steam.

Zengo raced past booths that handed out Kewpie dolls for balloons popped with darts. He could not believe that he was actually chasing the dude who had stared down from posters on his bedroom walls when he was a platypup. But Chase Mercy was no longer a movie star to Zengo. He was coward who was running from the law. He was no better than an illegal fish peddler.

Chase made a sharp turn onto the walkway that led to a dead end that housed the support beams for the ScreamerCoaster.

"Chase Mercy, stop right there!" Zengo shouted. "You have nowhere to run!"

Just then . . . *KA-BOOOOOOOM!*

Behind him, a tremendous explosion reverberated off the metal beams of the roller coaster. Zengo was nearly knocked off his webbed feet. He turned to see flames shooting up from above the Kalamazoo

City River of Dreams. His heart sank to the bottom of his tail. Could O'Malley have been near there?

Zengo looked back at Chase, now scaling the support beams of the roller coaster. Zengo wasn't surprised; he had seen Spy Masterson do things like this before, and everyone knew Chase Mercy did his own stunts. But what was the point of climbing up a roller coaster?

The answer came from above. A loud mechanical roar sounded overhead, and Zengo looked up to see a helicopter descending through the opening of the retractable roof. Every bit of this escape had been planned.

Except for the two detectives who had caught on to his plot. Zengo ran to the base of the ScreamerCoaster, threw off his jacket, and began to climb.

As he scrambled up, Zengo saw the flames of the raging fire on the other side of the Dome. He hoped O'Malley was okay. The thought of his partner gave Zengo the burst of energy he needed to zigzag up the maze of metal beams.

Soon Zengo was so high off the ground that any miscalculated move would send him plummeting to certain death. And he had certainly made a few miscalculated moves recently. But he also knew exactly why he was risking his life—to stand up for what was right and to protect the citizens of Kalamazoo City.

He felt strong and deter-mined as he stretched to grab the next bar, and then the one above that, going higher and higher until he was just a few feet below Chase Mercy, straddling the tracks at the highest part of the ScreamerCoaster. The helicopter was hover-ing directly above his head, the wind from its blades blowing his fur furiously.

"I'm sorry to have to run, Detective," Chase called back.

"But I've got an early shoot tomorrow, far away from here."

"Not so fast," yelled Zengo, who had finally reached up to feel the steel of the tracks. With one last, hard pull he hauled himself on top of the coaster. He was shocked to realize just how high up he was. His head spun and he almost threw up, right there.

The chopper lowered a rope ladder and Chase Mercy took a step toward it. Zengo pulled out his boomerang and held it in the ready position. He shouted, "Freeze! Do not take another step!"

Chase cocked his head and continued to reach

for the ladder.

Zengo flashed his boomerang. "Don't think for a second I won't use this, Chadwick Mickleheimer!"

The fleeing outlaw stopped dead in his tracks. Zengo knew it wasn't the boomerang that froze him. It was hearing his real name. Zengo took a step forward, his boomerang locked on target. "Mr. Mickleheimer, you are under arrest. Turn around slowly."

"There is no Chadwick Mickleheimer," shouted Chase Mercy. "He disappeared the moment I left this city. I'm no longer the kid nobody respected, the person everyone laughed at and called Squirt. My name is

Chase Mercy! I'm a star! And I'm showing the world that this town isn't worth anything."

"That's all over now, Chadwick," said Zengo, stepping forward. "You're a criminal, and you're running from the police. Paws on your head."

Chase Mercy looked back to the ladder, hanging a few feet away from him, then hung his head low and slowly placed his hands behind his head. Zengo's muscles relaxed the slightest bit at the sight of the criminal surrendering. He reached for his handcuffs, taking his eyes off Mercy for a moment, and as he did the movie star slugged Zengo across the bill, knocking the boomerang out of his hand and sending the detective plummeting off the tracks and into the abyss of night.

KALAMAZOO CITY DOME, 8:57 P.M.

Luckily just as he started to fall, Zengo was able to grab a section of tracks with one flipper. He held on for dear life, dangling hundreds of feet above the ground. He clamped his bill tight to take his mind off the searing pain shooting through his arm as it bore the full weight of his body.

Chase Mercy held on to the rope ladder with one hand as he stood above the flailing detective. "Nobody calls me by my real name, Detective. Nobody. Too bad there are no witnesses way up here; after you fall and I take off, there will be no one left to pin any of this on me!"

Chase stamped on the hand that gripped the tracks. Zengo could feel his bones getting crushed like potato chips in a tuna-fish sandwich. He steeled himself to ignore the pain, and maintained his grip. Meanwhile in one smooth motion, he locked one side of the handcuffs around one of Chase Mercy's ankles and secured the other side to one of the steel support beams.

"You're not going anywhere!" shouted Zengo.

Chase Mercy jerked at the handcuffs and realized that he was, indeed, not going anywhere. Enraged, he kicked Zengo with his free foot. The blow sent Zengo plummeting once again into the abyss of night.

Detective Rick Zengo saw his life flash before him as he fell. He thought about his parents. He thought about his grandfather. He thought about all the things he had hoped to do in his life. He looked at the tracks of the roller coaster as he plummeted toward them. He closed his eyes.

But he didn't hit the tracks. Instead, Zengo landed in a heap in one of the roller coaster's cars. His partner was beaming beside him. O'Malley had somehow caught him.

"What? Why? How?" said Zengo. "And besides—I thought you hated roller coasters!"

"*That's* the part that shocks you, kid?" said O'Malley, grinning madly at the success of his daring rescue.

"Well, your timing is impressive," said Zengo as he fumbled to secure his safety bar into place. "How did you do that, anyhow?"

"Simple physics!"

The car holding Zengo and O'Malley jerked from side to side as it turned a corner and began to creep up the steep incline to the last big drop.

"What are we going to do about Chase Mercy?" shouted Zengo, the wind flying in his face.

"What do you mean?" shouted O'Malley.

"He's handcuffed to the track up ahead. If we don't stop this coaster, our car is going to cream him!"

Zengo and O'Malley's car careened around the corner of the tracks. They were about two hundred feet away from Chase Mercy, who was frantically trying to free himself from the handcuffs.

Zengo began to panic. How would they ever stop in time? He had taken an oath to bring the corrupt to face justice at trial—not to flatten perps like hamburger patties.

Chase Mercy fell to his knees. They were a hundred feet away. Then fifty. Then twenty. Then ten.

Then just as they gave up hope, the detectives' car screeched to a halt, no more than a couple of feet from Chase Mercy.

"Sometimes you just have to know people who know people," said O'Malley. He pulled his walkie-talkie out of his breast pocket. "Nicely done, Professor Treeger.

Perfect timing, twice."

"Hey, roller coasters are my thing," said the professor, his voice crackling over the static of the radio.

"Hey, Chadwick, old friend," said O'Malley as he pulled out his badge and approached the crumpled figure. "You have the right to remain silent."

THE DOME PARKING LOT, 9:30 P.M.

Detectives Zengo and O'Malley each held one shoulder of the apprehended and disgraced movie star as they marched him in toward a waiting police car. They had their pick: the Dome parking lot was a sea of squad cars, all with red and blue lights flashing. It looked like a Fourth of July party at Bamboo.

In the back of one of the cars sat the disheveled perp with a large bite taken out of one ear. Mercy's lackey had been apprehended by O'Malley, though not before he had set the control center of the Kalamazoo City Dome to explode.

Luckily the flames from the explosion were fully extinguished by the Kalamazoo City Fire Department, who had, once again, made it to the Dome within minutes. The fire team was now loading its hoses back onto its trucks. The blaze at the Kalamazoo City River of Dreams had been put out, but the ride itself was destroyed. The animatronic figures inside were melted down to their metallic armatures.

Detectives Diaz and Lucinni were taking statements from witnesses, mostly park staff and party guests who were clustered in a roped-off section of the parking lot. This crowd was dressed to the nines and they were clearly rattled by the evening's events. Even tough guy Maurice Robertson and ice-cold Audrey Davis appeared shell-shocked.

Mayor Saunders was talking to Sergeant Plazinski, who stood near the cluster of squad cars with his arms crossed, and an ugly grimace on his face. The sergeant was clearly unimpressed with the city's highest elected official. As Zengo and O'Malley approached, Plazinski held up his hand to silence the mayor.

"Boys, you've done this city proud," he said.

"It was nothing," said Zengo.

"You're going to have to learn to take a compliment," continued the sergeant, scowling. "I don't dish them out too often."

"Thank you, sir," Zengo sheepishly responded.

"That's better. And O'Malley, your quick thinking has saved the day once again—"

"Thank you, sir," said O'Malley.

"You didn't let me finish. But the suit. What is up with this suit, O'Malley?" Plazinski took the collar of O'Malley's jacket into his webbed hand. "Polyester? Orange? Really, O'Malley! Is *this* how you dress up when I send you to a fancy party?"

"I think I'm pulling it off," said O'Malley.

"No. No, you're not. But you're a good cop." Plazinski stepped up to Chase Mercy and looked him directly in the eye. The handcuffed celebrity attempted to avert his gaze. "Chadwick Mickleheimer. I can't believe you'd do this to your own hometown. Take him away, boys."

Zengo and O'Malley handed Chase Mercy off to two uniformed cops. They hustled him into the back of their squad car and slammed the door before getting in themselves and driving off to put Chase Mercy behind bars.

"That was fine work back there," said Mayor Saunders to Zengo and O'Malley.

"Well, thank you, Mr. Mayor," said O'Malley. "But while we're all here together, we have a few questions for you."

"I have nothing to say," said Mayor Saunders as he buttoned his coat and began to step away. "There is some . . . business for me to attend to down at City Hall."

Derek Dougherty cut in. "I hate to interrupt," he said, though he obviously didn't. "Detectives, the mayor might not be so forthcoming right now, but I think that you'll enjoy my piece in tomorrow's newspaper. The mayor here hasn't been completely aboveboard about everything he's done to get this Dome built."

"What are you talking about?" inquired Mayor Saunders.

"Well, you see, the detectives here led me right into the offices of everybody in your Dream Team, as you like to call them. I couldn't get past security, but they could, and I snuck right in behind them. It's kind of what I do. And boy, did I find out some interesting things."

Zengo and O'Malley shared a look. The chameleon had been trailing them the whole time and they hadn't had a clue. Maurice and Audrey stood at attention.

"I did nothing illegal!" said Saunders.

"No. No, you didn't," said Derek. "But you rejected applications from reputable firms in Kalamazoo to make deals with these three Walhalla companies. It's easy to understand if you were trying to get the best people on the job, or if it would save the taxpayers money, but of course, that's not why you didn't choose a team from Kalamazoo, is it? None of them was your college girlfriend, eh, Mr. Mayor? None of them was a professor who once agreed to change your failing grade to a passing grade, am I right? And none of them was your old college roommate, either."

"W-w-what?" sputtered Mayor Saunders. "This is preposterous. Did they tell you this?"

"They didn't have to." Derek reached into his bag and produced a book: an old-looking Walhalla University yearbook. He flipped open to a page and pointed to a series of inscriptions there—inscriptions signed by Audrey Davis, Professor Treeger, and Maurice Robertson.

Plazinski raised an eyebrow. Saunders was

What a memorable year! Love you, Audrey

Hey Saunders. Let's Party over the summer. your bro – MAURICE!

Have a great summer! -Alice

Don't eva change! -Jordie

You were a fine light window! Captain Treger

flabbergasted. This wasn't going to end well for the mayor in the public eye.

"Anyhow," said Derek, slyly stepping away from the scene, "I have a story to write. Do look for it on the front page of tomorrow's edition. Of course, the story will be published below the feature on the unstable celebrities that the mayor has been bringing to town. A good evening to you all!" Derek bowed his head and with that, he was gone.

"Mr. Mayor," said Zengo.

"Huh?" said the befuddled mayor. He was clearly caught off-guard by the latest development. *He's probably already trying to plan out his political spin*, thought Zengo.

"Mr. Mayor, we're still going to need to get a written statement about this evening's events."

"Though we are very much looking forward to reading tomorrow's newspaper," said Plazinski, who wore a wide grin.

Corey O'Malley's phone rang. He took it out of his back pocket and looked at the screen. "It's my wife," he said.

"Take it," said Plazinski.

"Thanks." O'Malley flipped open his phone. *Leave it to O'Malley*, thought Zengo. Even his phone was out of date. It was surprising that his phone didn't also sport a cord and a rotary dial.

"Hey, Karen, yes, I'm fine. Zengo? Yes, he's okay,

208

too. Yup, it was a bit of a scare, but all is okay. Dinner? Um, we got to eat some food at the party, but honey, the food here was so tiny! Leftovers? I'll ask him." O'Malley put his webbed hand over the receiver and looked at Zengo.

"Yes!" said Zengo before O'Malley even said anything. The thought of a home-cooked meal by Mrs. O'Malley sounded like the perfect way to end this day.

"That's what I thought," said his partner. He said good-bye to his wife and hung up. "You did good tonight, rookie. Real good."

Zengo was so happy, for once he didn't even mind being called a rookie.

O'MALLEY HOUSE, 10:00 P.M.

Zengo and O'Malley walked in the front door just as Karen O'Malley was putting a reheated casserole on the dining-room table. The smell filled Zengo with happiness.

No wonder O'Malley had a little extra cushion, Zengo thought. If he had the chance to eat this well every day, he'd probably have trouble fitting into his suit jackets too.

"Now don't you look handsome!" said Mrs. O'Malley.

"Thanks, dear," said Corey, kissing his wife on the cheek.

"Oh, well you look nice too, honey, but I was talking to Rick." She blushed as she took Zengo's tuxedo jacket and hung it on the coatrack. "Come on in, boys. I hope you brought your appetites." She hugged her husband.

Karen busted the old man's chops, but it was clear to Zengo that she loved the heck out of him. It was clear too that she had been worried sick, based on the spread laid out on the table as well as the spotlessness of the house. When there is a cop in the family, it is impossible not to worry when he or she is out on assignment. With every local channel offering wall-to-wall coverage of the latest fiasco at the Dome, Zengo figured the O'Malley family had spent a pretty fretful evening. His mom was sure reassured to hear from him when he had called her on the way over to his partner's house.

Tonight even the kids seemed to have picked up on the mood of peace and relief. It was rarely this quiet in the O'Malley house. The youngest O'Malley, baby Lissy, was sound asleep in her crib down the hall. Vanessa was sitting at the table, her phone nowhere in sight. O'Malley's two boys, Jonathan and Declan, had been in front of the television, but leaped up and ran over to their dad as soon as they saw him. Declan gave him a huge hug. Corey kissed him on the forehead and patted him on the back.

"So," said O'Malley, taking his seat, "how was everyone's day?"

"Well, Blake and I got back together," said Vanessa.

"Oh. Good. I was worried," said the senior O'Malley, stuffing his bill with casserole. "And you, Declan, how was your day?"

"It was fine," said Declan. "I'm just glad you're home." O'Malley gave his younger son a smile and a wink and then turned to Jonathan, who Zengo was sure was hoping to avoid this question altogether.

"What about you, Johnny, short day at school, eh?"

Zengo wondered if the kid would correct his dad about his name as he usually did. But there was something more important on Jonathan's mind.

"Dad, I made a mistake, and I'm sorry," Jonathan said.

"Well, you did, and you're never skipping school again, son. There will be consequences." O'Malley may have just taken down the city's number one suspect, but at the end of the day, he was a dad first.

"Well, yes, that was a mistake, too—but I wasn't

213

talking about that," Jonathan said.

O'Malley put down his fork.

"Dad, I'm sorry for calling Chase Mercy my hero."

O'Malley wiped his mouth. "That's okay, kid. You don't need to apologize for that." He patted his son on the back, and Jonathan smiled.

Jonathan seemed to have more to say. "Dad . . ." he began.

Zengo's phone buzzed with a news alert. He checked the screen. The headline read MAYOR SAUNDERS RESIGNS. "O'Malley, we might want to turn on the television."

The screen came on to the sound of the "Special Bulletin" music. But it wasn't Mayor Saunders whose face filled the screen. Instead, Frank Pandini Jr. was holding a press conference.

"Turn it up, would you, buddy?" O'Malley asked Jonathan. Jonathan ran over to the remote control and turned up the volume. Everyone crowded around to watch.

Pandini stood behind a podium emblazoned with the Kalamazoo City skyline. The magnate was dressed in his signature white tuxedo. He was clearly in command of the crowd as he stood powerfully and confidently, waiting for them to be silent.

Probably just getting ready to take credit for the mayor stepping down and everything that happened at the Dome tonight, thought Zengo.

Pandini cleared his throat and adjusted the microphone. "Thank you all for joining me here on this historic evening," he began.

Zengo and O'Malley shared a look. O'Malley's cocked eyebrow signaled what Zengo was already thinking.

"I, along with everyone in Kalamazoo City, am completely shocked and dismayed by Mayor Saunders's sudden resignation. We will all read the exposé in tomorrow's newspaper, but it's clear to the former mayor now that he can't pull the wool over this fair city's eyes and expect to get away with it. It got too hot in the kitchen for Saunders, and he made some mistakes. I, however, am used to being in some very hot kitchens. You may have stopped in to one of my many fine establishments across the city, like Black and White, or Bamboo. I've spent many hours in the back of those hot kitchens perfecting the cuisine and coaching my staff to make sure their service to our customers is second to none. And I do believe that my reputation for excellence speaks for itself. I care very much for this city, and I would like to bring my own unique brand of service to every single citizen of Kalamazoo City, even those who have yet to stop by Roar, or the newly renovated Kalamazoo Coliseum.

"To that end, tonight I am officially announcing my candidacy for mayor of Kalamazoo City in the special election to replace our outgoing leader."

The cameras flashed and the reporters immediately began to hammer Pandini with questions. But the mogul just flashed his winning smile and waved to the cameras before stepping off the stage.

"The mayor called it quits?" exclaimed Karen.

"I suppose it was inevitable," O'Malley observed. "Derek had dug up some pretty damaging dirt about him and the Dream Team."

"It's not the mayor's resignation that worries me," said Zengo, leaning back in his chair. "It's Pandini. Saunders hasn't even left the mayor's mansion and Frank is already measuring for drapes."

"Dad, do you think he has a chance of winning?" asked Declan.

"This is Kalamazoo City, son," said O'Malley, though the look he gave Zengo was anything but reassuring. "Everybody has a chance of winning here."

ACKNOWLEDGMENTS

Many thanks to everyone at Walden Pond Press and HarperCollins Children's Books who, once again, hit the streets of Kalamazoo City with me: Jordan Brown, Kellie Celia, Debbie Kovacs, Tom Forget, Jenna Lisanti, Mrs. de la Sun, and the many others working behind the scenes. Thanks to Rebecca Sherman, Eddie Gamarra, and Deb Shapiro for being a part of my Squad. Thanks to Joey Weiser and Michele Chidester, who blocked the graytones into my illustrations for this book. Thank you to officers Chris Zengo and Corey McGrath, who continue to inspire me with their bravery and service. And above all, thank you to my girls, Gina, Zoe, and Lucy.

JARRETT J. KROSOCZKA

is the author and illustrator of the Lunch Lady graphic novel series, a two-time winner of the Children's Choice Book Award, as well as many picture books. He can be heard on "The Book Report with JJK," his radio segment on SiriusXM's Kids Place Live. Jarrett lives in Northampton, Massachusetts, with his wife, two daughters, and their pug, Ralph Macchio. You can visit him online at www.studiojjk.com.

For exclusive information on your favorite authors and artists, visit www.authortracker.com.

Also available as an ebook.

Zengo and O'Malley will return in . . .

PLATYPUS POLICE SQUAD: LAST PANDA STANDING

The Kalamazoo City mayoral race is heating up, and Frank Pandini Jr. has been threatened by a mysterious assailant. He requests a special Platypus Police Squad protection detail: Detective Rick Zengo. Can Zengo get to the bottom of the attacks—without O'Malley backing him up?